MW00814850

Drawn
From Life

For Patricia Powell

Ford and Chrysler

From his stubby point of view each make of car had its own personality. He would stand, brown eyes at headlight level, puckering up for a smooch of Mommy's 1940 Dodge or narrowing his lips to a thin line to match the toothless smile of Gramma's '42 Chrysler. But Grandmother's '39 black Ford had a fussy swept up mustache that caused him to squint and wrinkle his nose.

He was Pete. He had been born in a year of no new cars, only jeeps, tanks, and half tracks. Before the war, before Pete was born, Daddy had broken his family tradition of Fords and bought himself an Oldsmobile. Pete did not recall Daddy ever having gone away to fight but did have a cloudy memory of the silver blue Olds resting on blocks in the garage and of himself trying to spin its sluggish tires when he was not yet two.

Grandmother, who had the Ford, lived close to them in their village near Lake Michigan, but Gramma with the Chrysler had her place by the Mississippi one hundred and thirty-two miles west. She had retired there long ago. Pete told her he too would retire there when he was old.

The land between the lake and the river was Illinois, and there in Pete's travels every possible make of car would pass, coming and going, and he could identify them all. Shortly after his second birthday, sitting on the curb in front of his house, Pete had witnessed the first post-war models roll by. Mommy and Daddy were astonished when he recognized the '46 Chrysler from the way it had opened its tight-lipped '42 smile and now showed rows of teeth the same as Pete could do at last.

One day his Ford grandfather showed up in a new Mercury. It had a broad mustache brushed down across its upper lip. Pete could discern the family resemblances, for Fords and Mercurys belonged together the way Chryslers and Dodges did. But Mommy had her Dodge and Daddy had his Oldsmobile, so what kind of car would Pete ever have for himself?

Neglected

"Mommy, I think you should get a Nash."

Pete was hanging around the kitchen while she washed the strawberries and sliced their tops off.

"There isn't a Nash dealer nearby, Pete. I feel more comfortable having a dealer in the village."

"Daddy will buy you a Nash in Chicago and make it a big surprise."

"You suggest it to him then," said Mommy.

Pete did not expect Daddy to approve of such a plan, but he would try. Nashes were rarer than Dodges, and that was why he wanted Mommy to drive one. Pete never wanted his family to be like everyone else. His parents said they wondered why he was so fascinated with the unpopular and the neglected.

"You know what you could do?" said Mommy as she rolled the strawberries about on the dishtowel to dry

3

them off. Pete's brown eyes at counter level were open wide, but he said nothing. "You could draw a Nash ad. Maybe you'll even convince Daddy."

Unlike most of her suggestions to get him peacefully sitting in a corner out of the way, this one struck Pete as appealing. Soon he was on the back porch with his crayons and manila paper, and when Daddy came home he presented him with a portrait of the bug-like car, dark green against a light blue sky with "Nash for 1949" across the top and at the bottom the price, $99.

"That's a Bathtub Nash!" Daddy said. "I'd know it even if you didn't say so. You're good, Pete."

"It's an Airflyte Nash," Pete corrected him. If he had been surer of his spelling he would have labeled it more precisely. Now as his sales pitch he added, "The seats turn into beds."

"Just what you'll need when you get to high school, buddy."

"But Mommy would like one now to replace her old Dodge."

Daddy looked down at him carefully. Pete knew he could tell it was not what Mommy actually had said. "I've been leaning more toward a Plymouth, Pete. They've got a spiffy yellow convertible in the showroom. Can't you see Mommy driving a convertible?"

Which was what she ended up with. But the ad for the Nash remained tacked up in the back stairs, and Pete began drawing other cars. Mommy would take him down to the parking lot behind the Village Hall, and he would spend a couple of hours happily sketching while she did the shopping.

Hermes

The dusty green cover of the phone book bore a finely etched drawing of Mercury, the Messenger of the Gods. Pete called him Naked Nerk. He was the first naked man in Pete's acquaintance. Recently Mommy had been reading him Greek myths at bedtime from a book with woodcuts in bold black and white, and there was Mercury again but now known as Hermes, which somehow sounded nakeder and more beautiful. The cape or cloak he wore clasped at his neck managed in the illustrations to fall right in front of his equipment, or else he was leaping with his winged sandals through the air with one long muscular leg stretched forward, concealing what would have stood out if you could see him from the other side.

Hermes was on a voyage to the Underworld to bring Persephone home to visit her mother. Pete liked the story, even the scary picture of dark-browed Pluto holding the slender girl in his huge arms. But when Mommy left the room and he was supposed to be asleep Pete opened the book again and traced in the faint glow of his nightlight the supple limbs of leaping Hermes then rubbed his finger along the smooth naked thighs of Hermes standing at the gates of the Underworld begging admittance from the three-headed dog.

Pete knew how good it was to look at Hermes but did not know why. When he leaned his head on Mommy's lap while she read to him, he knew he should not pay any particular attention to the Hermes pictures. For her sake he would even ask to look especially at the one of sorrowing Demeter as if it were his favorite instead. It also was beautiful, and it stayed with him too, her sad eyes gazing at the dry earth that might never grow flowers again. Mommy once asked him why he liked that picture so much and why he chuckled so over the picture of wrinkly Charon with his scrawny bare bottom poling across the Styx. Pete knew it was fine to laugh at Charon's old bottom but that he should not notice Hermes's beautiful one, and he knew Mommy liked it when he said the reason he felt sorry for Demeter was that the picture made him feel her feeling. That was true. Pete already worried about things he might lose some day.

God

"We're getting Sarah," Mommy said. "Your grandparents don't need her anymore. They really only need Doreen."

"But where would she live?" Pete asked.

"With us. The room off the back stairs."

"But there's no bathroom."

"She'll use the basement john, and Daddy's going to have a sink put in her room."

Pete was afraid of Sarah being there all the time. Whenever they visited Grandmother and Grandfather she was strict with him.

"Keep out of Mommy's hair," she said. Mommy was going to have a baby.

"She'll be a help when your brother or sister gets here," Mommy explained. She still had not made up her mind about the baby. Pete hoped she would choose

7

a sister because he felt more relaxed around girls. "Sarah has always liked you, Pete. She says you're the easiest six-year-old boy she ever met."

Pete knew that was a compliment. Mommy often complained about his cousin Maurice, Aunt Helena's son who was nine. "Thank God they moved to New York," Mommy said. It was one of the few times he heard her mention God other than to say that as a family we do not believe in him, he is something other people have come up with to keep themselves under control, but we don't need that. "Besides, the Greek gods are more fun," Pete remembered her adding with a wink.

Pete had seen the gruesome paintings of Jesus Christ in Mommy and Daddy's art books. Sarah believed Jesus Christ was God. Pete had never wanted to touch Jesus Christ the way he did Hermes. Jesus Christ looked sick and pale and not very friendly.

"There's one thing about Sarah I have to warn you of," Mommy said. "She's not just a polite Christian like your grandparents."

How had Mommy known Pete was thinking of Jesus Christ? Sometimes she seemed to hear thoughts in his head he did not want to say aloud.

"And that means she has a way of not keeping her religion to herself. So if she starts telling you about God watching you every minute or about what you should or shouldn't do or you'll go to hell, don't take her serious-ly. I don't want any of her Jesus talk getting you scared. Daddy and I don't want any of that guilt and morality crap in your life," Mommy said with a little laugh because she had gotten excited and said *crap*.

But it meant Pete would never forget what she had told him.

In the Garage

He liked visiting Gramma, especially now that his little brother took up so much of his mom's time and left him more on his own for the summer. Out there by the Mississippi there was plenty to do. After Gramma made him toast with strawberry jam and he drank his milk and then his orange juice, which bit into his milky gums in a pleasant way, he always began by going to find Lemuel in the garage.

Lemuel was quiet and slow, and that made him less scary than other men. He had a crewcut and was hand-some like a cowboy on television. Though he was two years older than Pete's dad he seemed younger because he wore blue jeans and was skinny and his arms were smooth. Lemuel's room was up above the two-car garage, an attic with a peaked ceiling, and there was a potbelly stove he did not need in summer and a hot plate to make his coffee on when he got up before anyone else was ever awake.

Pete had discovered that Lemuel slept naked. Back in June, excited to be there at Gramma's, Pete had woken up before sunrise. He wanted to see Lemuel, who had been asleep when they arrived late the night before, so he crept out and across the wet grass to the garage's side door. He waited awhile on the steps leading up to Lemuel's room. Then he heard a big yawn and some nose blowing, so he climbed up and knocked, which caused the crooked door to swing open on its own.

Lemuel sat up in bed with no shirt on and said, "Look who got here at last!" Pete was unsure, but Lemuel patted the bed and said, "Set yourself down, Pete. Hold on a minute. First I got to piss."

So with Pete standing at the foot of his bed Lemuel turned the blue bedspread down, swung his legs around, and reached for the chamber pot. His equipment was sticking out in front bigger than Pete had ever seen one. Lemuel leaned down and bent it to aim into the pot, and as he turned his bare brown back there came a loud splashing sound Pete had remembered all summer. He watched Lemuel's pale white bottom as it sat there on the white sheet. Then Lemuel set the pot down, swung his legs back onto the bed, and pulled the bedspread over himself, but from the way it bunched up Pete could see where Lemuel's equipment lay back against his tummy. Standing there Pete told him about school and his new little brother, and eventually Lemuel stood up too and pulled on his jeans. Pete looked away that time but later wished he had not.

He never managed to wake up so early again on any of their visits and especially not on this long one in August when his dad had stayed home to work. Baby John got his mom up in the dark, which also woke Pete and caused him to sleep even later in the mornings. One morning only Gramma was up when he came down. She said she had a treat planned. Lemuel was going to drive them up to Horse River State Park for a campaign picnic with Governor Stevenson, who was running for president, and Pete might get to shake his hand.

She packed a wicker basket and they snuck out, leaving Mom and John napping. The old Chrysler pulled up by the kitchen door.

Pete was about to climb into the back seat when Lemuel said, "Come set here with me."

They took the county road up Horse Valley. Gramma was asking Lemuel whether after ten years she might not be due for a new car. She would wait to see what the '53 DeSotos looked like. Pete watched the hilly cornfields rippling along in their rows. He was on his way to meet maybe the next president of the United States but was more excited to be sitting beside Lemuel. When he looked at him he tried not to look too long. Pete knew it was strange to be so curious, but Mom had told him he was someone who thought with his eyes and that was what made him an artist.

Madly for Adlai

Gramma and Pete wore their big blue buttons back from the picnic. Lemuel promised he would vote Democratic but said he had no use for slogans and all that hoopla. He had shared their lunch but mostly talked to a farmer he knew sitting with his fat wife on the next blanket.

Gramma was encouraging Pete to draw a portrait of Governor Stevenson now that he had shaken his hand, so Pete set about recapturing the event in his sketch-book. Governor Stevenson's face came across as kindly and wise, a small gentle mouth and the bald forehead he was famous for. He was reaching down to shake a boy's hand, but you only saw the boy from behind, the blue and white stripes of his shirt, some wavy brown hair, and a small outstretched hand. Then Pete tried it again and felt he improved on it by making Governor Stevenson's eyes squint in a sparkly way and opening his mouth up more, which made the nose seem even larger. "Would he like this one better?" he asked Gramma.

"He looks just like himself in it," she said, "but he might prefer the first one. It's more flattering."

So Pete kept the second and with Gramma's help sent the first to the campaign headquarters at the county seat. A month later when he was back home he got a letter addressed to Master Peter Dabney. It said, "My dear Peter, Thank you very much for your excellent drawing. It will always remind me of a happy day in my life. Sincerely yours, Adlai E. Stevenson."

"It's his actual signature," Mom said. "Imagine taking the time to write to a non-voter."

"It's made him a Democrat for life," said Dad.

"I trust he's already that," said Mom.

Pete stared at the letter while they talked. He had never received a typed letter before, only little notes from Gramma and cards on his birthday. The "my dear Peter" made him feel good. He could not imagine General Eisenhower calling him "my dear Peter." Sarah had an "I Like Ike" button on her coat and told Pete how he saved the world from the Germans, which was more than the Egghead could do. Pete did not credit her politics any more than he did her talk about Jesus saving the world from sin.

A Single Line

He began drawing more people. They were harder than cars because they changed their expressions. The same face could look friendly or mean depending on what Pete did with its lips and eyebrows. It could look happy or sad or smart or stupid, but then there were even more things Pete could see in the faces he drew, so that it was no longer possible to put it into one word. There was the drawing of his cousin Maurice, who had come from New York City for Christmas. He looked like a sneaky boy pretending to be nice who was acting like he knew what he was doing but you could tell he was unsure inside. Mom loved that drawing and showed it to Aunt Helena, who said in a serious voice, "Pete, you have a real gift. It's a bit scary." Pete looked worriedly up at her. "I mean in a good way, kiddo."

But in the spring Pete found he could finally draw someone beautiful. It made him so excited when he had done it he did not show it to Mom or Dad or anyone. It was a simple line drawing of a boy in his swimming class named Bill, who wore a tight kind of bathing suit instead of the saggy one Pete wore, and on the sides it was held together by four elastic strips so you could see the pink skin three times between the bands of blue. Pete did not know Bill more than to say "hi" to. He never got to be his buddy when they paired up. Alone in his room with his sketchbook Pete was surprised how well he remembered the way Bill looked, and how easily he could make a single line with his thinnest charcoal that looked exactly like the curve of Bill's leg. Bill's last name Rice rhymed with Gramma's last name Tice and made Pete feel secretly even closer to him. He would rather have been a Tice than a Dabney. He felt more like one.

He kept his drawing of Bill Rice in a special envelope in the drawer of his bedside table and tried not to look at it too often so it would stay a surprise.

Crash Test

He was at Bobby's house with its backyard pool. They had been playing crash test with Bobby's car collection, a thing Pete would never allow with his, and then they felt hot enough to swim so Bobby's mother let Pete borrow a pair of Bobby's trunks and they spent the rest of the afternoon in and out of the water.

Bobby shot cars off the diving board, and Pete with flippers dived for them. He caught the brand new '54 Eldorado before it hit the bottom, but even with goggles he was usually not fast enough. When Pete surfaced Bobby would check if his mother was around and then call him words like *fuckhole* and *bumwad*. They were good friends because Pete never took him too seriously.

When they went up to Bobby's room to change Bobby took two huge fluffy maroon towels out of the linen closet, and they each wrapped up in one to dry off after dropping their soggy trunks on the bathroom tiles. Bobby was doing the Sheik of Araby routine with a smaller white towel around his head, but soon it fell off. Pete held his own towel tighter when they started wrestling on the bedroom carpet. Then Bobby jumped up and held his towel open for a flash. His wiener was sticking out, and Pete was afraid Bobby would see his doing the same thing. Bobby started pulling at Pete's towel and trying to roll him out of it. Bobby's towel was slipping off and soon fell away entirely leaving only the one towel between their bodies. They could feel each other.

Then Bobby jumped up again and started dancing around the room with his little thing flapping in front until they heard his mother calling them down for sundaes. Bobby took advantage of the pause to roll Pete out of his towel. "I saw your dick, I saw your butt," he sang.

"Well, I saw yours plenty," said Pete.

"I wanted you to," said Bobby with a snap of his hip that caused his dick to wiggle. "Yours is bigger," he said.

"No, it's not," said Pete getting quickly into his underpants. That tingling he had felt from being all cold in the swimming pool and then wrapped up in that soft towel had left him. He felt hot and sweaty again.

Storm Approaching

Pete sat out in Gramma's meadow and sketched. He was in the dappled shade of the great spreading oak tree along the edge of where Lemuel always kept a mown swath, but the meadow itself was high in grass and fluttering cabbage whites. The hot summer air was blowing across from Iowa and moving on east bringing thunderstorms surely by sunset. Pete loved the sense of weather building up to do something. He wanted his sketches today to catch that. It amazed him how he could draw an invisible thing like a breeze by the way he drew leaves and grasses, a dance in the delicate tips of the oak leaves, a turning in the elms, a twirl of tufts. Everything he made in stillness actually moved.

Leaning back against the oak trunk and looking up into the branches Pete thought of the immense weight reaching out above him. It would take Lemuel a day to chop up and stack so much wood. It was a whole truck-load over his head. He wondered if he could draw weight the way he drew the invisible breeze or the lightness of butterflies over the meadow or sunshine on the river. He turned a page and tried again.

The dancing turning leaves might be light, but above them or behind them, or maybe not even there yet, was something very heavy. He did not want to draw a thundercloud. He wanted to give the sense of thunder on its way, and maybe a lightning strike and a huge limb splitting from the trunk, ripping, crashing. His mind got quite crazy when he tried to think these things out, so he just let his right hand move and smudged here and there with his left. He was getting closer to it.

He knew when it was time to run back down the hill with his sketchbook under his arm before the rain hit. Mom and John were telling stories on the screen porch, and Gramma was clanking pots in the kitchen.

Green Mansions

His book report was on *Green Mansions*. His mom had been sure he would love it, and he did for the first half, but then it got confusing. The color illustrations helped. He brought the book to English, and Miss Ingram was surprised. Other kids brought shorter books like *Light in the Forest* and *The Raft* and *Good Morning, Miss Dove* from their Young Readers Club, but Pete brought this heavy old Heritage Press edition from his parents' shelves.

He made a mistake when he opened to the picture of Rima entirely in the nude. Despite the illustration Pete had not thought of her that way when he was reading the book. She was the Bird Girl. He imagined her in a cloak of bright feathers without such pale skin or her bosoms showing.

The boys hooted when he held up the open book not realizing which page it was on, and the girls all got mad, so Miss Ingram stepped in. "If you people are so immature," she said, "as to get silly over a drawing of a naked woman then you don't belong in sixth grade."

Marc put on a harmless face and asked, "What if it was a naked man with his wiener showing?"

"*Wiener* is a fifth-grade term, mister," said Miss Ingram. "In sixth grade we call it a penis." Everyone shut up. They could not believe Miss Ingram had said *penis* out loud. In the silence it was hard for Pete to start again to explain what he liked about this long book. It was not so much the story of the South American jungle as the ideas it gave him for pictures to draw. That was his problem in English. His thoughts wandered to different ways of seeing things and made him forget the words on the pages.

In the lunch line the boys were still kidding him about his book report, so he went to an empty table at the far end and sat with his back to the room. It would have been seen as cool if Marc had held up the picture of Rima, but because everyone knew Pete was not trying to make trouble he was only seen as a dork. He heard the scraping of chair legs and looked up to see that boy Russ taking the opposite seat. They had never sat together at lunch.

"My parents have that same book," Russ said, "only an edition with woodcuts instead. They're more evocative."

"Did you read it too?" Pete asked.

"Not yet, but I know all my parents' books from leafing through. I'm reporting on *How Green Was My Valley*. It's about Wales. No, I don't mean whales," he added with a breathy H.

Their sloppy joes were getting all over their fingers. Luckily Russ had grabbed a pile of paper napkins and passed one across to Pete. Russ was new to the class but despite being smart had immediately fit in with the athletes because he was tall and fast though not handsome or cool. "My parents give me a lot of art books," Pete said.

Russ had something more interesting to say. "My parents keep two volumes called *The Psychology of Sex* on the highest shelf. There's a chapter on auto-eroticism. When I was younger I supposed it was about cars."

Pete looked up hopefully. Could Russ possibly share his obsession? "I like to draw cars," he said.

But Russ did not hear him and said, "I'm embarrassed by what once I didn't know." Pete laughed with him. "And there's also a chapter on Inversion. There's things in that book you wouldn't believe like actual masochists. You should come over sometime and I'll show you when my mom is out. Other kids would find it too hard to read."

"I'm a slow reader," Pete admitted.

"But you're different," said Russ. "I can see you like the real weird stuff like me."

They moved on to their chocolate-frosted brownies.

Little Brother

John thought his big brother was fascinating and did not realize that Pete found John the fascinating one. In school Pete was studying how the human being progressed from a seed in an egg inside the womb to an old person about to die, but John's day-by-day growth process was not as orderly.

"He doesn't want to sleep now, Mom," Pete said when she kept going in and out of John's small room to stop his whining.

"You sit up with him then," she snapped back.

It was not like his mom to snap, so Pete was worried about her. "All right," he said.

"I've read him every story he has and even made some up."

"I don't mind," Pete said cheerfully and went in to sit on the rug next to his brother's low bed with the safety railings.

24

"No story from you," said John.

"We'll talk, then," Pete proposed. "I'll ask you questions."

John, who was nearly five, nodded skeptically.

"Do you know how you grow?"

John stared at Pete then cautiously shook his head.

"You put food in your mouth and it goes down to your stomach, which is spongy on the inside and sucks out vitamins and minerals and puts them into your blood to build your body. Then what's left travels through your large and small intestine and comes out as poop."

"How?" John asked.

"When you were younger it came out whenever it got there, but now you hold it in till you're on the pot."

"But how does it move?"

"Because of gravity," Pete said somewhat unsure of himself. "You put the food in up here, and it comes out down there."

"Is it still alive?"

"It was alive before it got cooked, but now it's a waste product," Pete explained.

Then John confessed that he talked to his poops. Pete had thought he heard him in there talking. "First I put down toilet paper on the water," John said, "so they won't splash. Then I say, 'Hello, poop, I'm John.'"

"Does it talk back?" Pete asked seriously.

"It has a voice," said John. "It says, 'I am Grampa Poop, and I am smelly.'" The poop voice was much slower than John's normal way of speaking. "'Now here comes Gramma Poop!'" said the voice, then John's own voice continued, "So the next one lands and says, 'Hi, Grampa, nice to see you.'" Her voice was more of a chortle. Then John asked with a sleepy whine, "But where do poops actually come from?"

"They're made from whatever you eat, John, I already told you."

"I make them?" John said with sudden wonder. Then he told Pete he wanted to think about this by himself so Pete could leave.

Mom gave him an apologetic smile when he shut John's door behind him and settled into a chair across the living room from her. He picked up the issue of *Life* he had been looking at before supper and found the picture of young King Hussein of Jordan standing in his uniform with all the other Arab kings in their robes. Pete was drawn to King Hussein's shy face. It looked overwhelmed.

In the evenings Pete never felt as happy as he did before supper when he first got home from school and smelled the cigarette smoke in the living room and heard the crackling fire and his mom let him have the green olive out of her martini.

Virginity

Pete was worried the counselors might come back early from their meeting, so he stayed in his upper bunk and watched. The other boys held their flashlights against their palms so only a glow of red shone through the plastic shields. Someone would flash his light around the cabin and everyone would gasp and pound the kid who did it. Then there would be more snickers and whispers and Pete could see their dicks in the faint light again. Lonny in the bunk below him was pretending to be asleep, but even Pete's best friend Nick had gotten down from his upper bunk and joined the circle in his underpants. Nelson made him take them off if he expected to be part of it.

Then came another flash across the ceiling, and Pete burrowed under his pillow but kept watching because Bruce had said he was going to fuck Nelson. No one had ever done that before. They had only jacked off.

Bruce was not one of the cool guys, just a freckled kid with a long curved-up boner he liked to wave around, but Nelson was the coolest in the whole cabin, the nicest and handsomest and the best at sports. He put Butchwax in his hair. Pete figured Nelson wanted to test how far Bruce would go. None of this felt at all like last week's trip to Tahquamenon Falls when it was cold and rainy and Danny had snuggled up with Pete in the back of the truck and hugged him supposedly to stay warm or when for skinny dip Pete was Allen's buddy and they had to hold onto each other on the diving float when buddy call came.

Nelson was standing on the floor with his bare feet apart and his hands holding the rail of his upper bunk. Bruce was now right behind him with his boner. Nelson's butt looked red in the light. Pete had an excruciating boner himself and pressed it against the sheet so it would not shoot off on its own. He would never be able to forget what he was seeing.

They were all whispering. Fred made his ape noise. Geoff, who won the jack-off contest, squealed, "Do it! Do it!" Then the round tip of Bruce's boner touched between Nelson's butt cheeks, and Pete imagined the warm poking feeling that must have made Nelson yelp and jump aside.

Everyone was disappointed. Bruce still stood there ready, but Pete knew the moment had passed. He did not think Nelson had been testing Bruce after all. Pete decided he must truly have wanted to see what being fucked felt like but then got scared.

Soon everyone but Pete and Lonny was jacking off again. Then later they took turns pissing out the corroded screen into the weeds behind the cabin. Pete would wait till they were all asleep and then sneak outside to take his own pee onto those crinkled-up smelly weeds.

Death of a Beauty

It was a free hour when most boys liked to storm around in the woods bombarding each other with pine cones, but Pete and Nick were alone in the cabin on their top bunks. Nick had borrowed Pete's already shaggy copy of Joe H. Wherry's *Complete 1955 Road Tests* to compare it with his own 1956 compendium. Pete had brought his last twelve months of *Motor Trend* to re-study carefully.

He came once more upon the small photo at the bottom of a page that showed a car transporter holding four '55 Kaisers under the title "Death of a Beauty." There was something trusting and brave in their headlights and grilles as they were being shipped from the factory. Pete read the caption over it: "Loading here for their last voyage are the final Kaisers to be built in the U.S. Darrin's style leading sedans will go to Argentina may resume building there in '56." From the way it was written Pete was unable to tell if those four cars were themselves going to Argentina or were simply the last ones built here, and he had yet to find any confirmation of the new models from Argentina.

He read the caption to Nick, who then looked up *Kaiser* in Wherry's book and from his bunk read excerpts across to Pete. "'It has style, real lines that do not need chrome plastered all over them to create a sensation.' I know it's still your favorite, Dabney," Nick said. "I mean I know it was a great design, but it couldn't compete in the market with Ford and GM. That's just being realistic. Hey, listen, Wherry says, 'Rumors of impending doom are unfounded.' That shows what *he* knew."

Pete was sad all over again. He could not say anything.

"I'm sorry, Dabney," Nick said. "I know how much you love your Kaisers and your Frazers. But your Nashes are going in with Hudson, and Studebaker with Packard. Maybe they'll make it."

"There's nothing in '56 as beautiful as the '55 Kaiser," Pete said with resignation. He took his summer sketchbook off the shelf and started to draw a tribute, but for once he could not put anything on paper and just stared at his few scribbles.

"Hey, man," said Nick. He was a good friend.

Then their counselor stomped in slamming the screen door and barked, "What are you lazy fairies lying around inside for? This is free hour, not nap time, guys."

James and Sal

The most private and secret story in Pete's life was the story of Sal Mineo and James Dean. Pete had seen *Rebel Without a Cause* in seventh grade. His friend Russ's parents had dropped them off not caring what movie they were going to. Pete never told his mom and dad. He had always liked Natalie Wood on TV, so he pretended to Russ that she was why he wanted to see the movie. He knew that James Dean was already dead, and it was almost creepy to find him so beautiful to look at. But after seeing the movie Pete made James Dean not so much someone who had died but a character in a story, and the story had to do with Sal Mineo as well while Natalie Wood pretty much faded out.

At first Pete was himself neither Sal nor James but made them both up in his head. If he thought about it he was certainly more Sal though, because it was James, in the form of his pillow, whom he leaned into at night and held close and talked to. His version of James had never died in a crash at all.

Russ had actually taped up a photo of James Dean from *Life* magazine on his bedroom wall. Russ said he was the coolest looking guy ever. Pete stuck to his Natalie Wood story with Russ, but when he was alone he began to feel all the more like Sal Mineo, how he was so devoted to James in the movie. Pete knew he was short and compact like Sal even if his hair did not curl quite as much. He would never be loose limbed and tough like James Dean.

Pete avoided thinking about the fatal car crash, but then Dad took him and John to see the stock car races. It was something for Dad to do with the boys without Mom. Pete had been excited to see again all the old cars that nowadays passed by so rarely, cars from before the war. The races made him nervous though when the cars got dented up, and Pete felt terrible when everyone in the stands cheered if one got entirely smashed. Then came the Demolition Derby, and Pete said to his dad, "I think John might get too scared. I think we should leave."

Pete knew whenever John had a crying fit Dad left him to Mom, and indeed Dad now said, "I bet you'd rather go look over the cars out back behind the stands, eh, buddy?"

So with the roarings and screechings and cheers behind them Pete and his brother walked with their dad along a row of rattletraps awaiting their turn to get smashed. "That's a '34 Airflow DeSoto," Pete told John, who kept turning around toward the lights they were moving away from. To Pete the car seemed to have no nose. Its tall narrow mouth was open wide to the eyebrows. "They considered it streamlined," he told John. "It was ahead of its time."

"Pete, do you remember how you could identify every make on the road when you were three?" his dad said.

Pete felt proud of himself. He was wondering how much it would cost to buy one of those old cars and save it. He imagined being Sal Mineo driving very safely around Los Angeles in an Airflow DeSoto with James Dean beside him. He was aware he could never tell these secret stories to his dad or to Russ or to anyone.

Songs of Catullus

In eighth grade Russ founded the Orff Club dedicated to listening to the music of Carl Orff. Russ had first heard Orff on FM and now owned three LPs of his own. They were sung mostly in Latin, and on the back of the one called *Catulli Carmina* was a blank space in the translation. He figured that meant it was sexy.

Pete was happy to spend afternoons in Russ's room listening. The James Dean picture had now been filed in a bottom desk drawer with other things Russ had clipped over the years. Pete was leafing through them while they played Orff. There were pictures of musclemen from the backs of comic books but also girdle and bra ads and dozens of Nancy and Sluggo strips from the *Sun-Times*. Russ loved their stupid jokes better than *Mad Magazine*.

Russ had his parents' Latin dictionary and was at his desk translating the record jacket. "'O your snakelike tongue,'" he said after flipping a lot of pages. "'Bite me, kiss me,' whoo hoo, this is crazy!"

"Why would it say 'bite me'?" Pete asked.

"You know, love bites, not bite bites."

Pete had never thought of biting anyone as sexy. When they talked dirty at camp no one had said anything about wanting a girl to bite him.

"'O your breasts, your soft breasts, sweet and firm, *gemina poma*.' Twin fruits! Whoo!"

Pete did not like the fierce rhythm coming from Russ's portable record player. He preferred Buddy Holly or the Everly Brothers or Harry Belafonte's *Calypso* album. He put up with Orff for Russ's sake.

"'My hand is eager to take—' or 'grab.' I'll make it 'grab them,'" Russ said leaning over the dictionary. "This is getting me aroused. Listen how it goes here: *'Mea manus est cupida, cupida, cupida—'* That means 'eager, eager, eager'— And then here, listen!"

A man's wild voice on the record shouted *"O vos pupillae horridulae!"* as if he was about to rape someone.

"Wow!" said Russ. He reached over to lift the needle. "Wait." He turned back to his desk. Pete could tell he was feeling himself up through his jeans, which had gotten bulgy, while he flipped pages with his other hand. "It means, it means—wow! 'O your protruding nipples!'"

"That's why they couldn't translate it," Pete said. He hoped Russ would not want to jack off. He could never jack off in front of Russ, who was his best friend, though he had done it with Marc.

36

Sex seemed to be everywhere now. That Christmas his Aunt Helena had sent him a Jayne Mansfield hot water bottle from New York City. When he opened it he guffawed as if it was the craziest thing he had ever seen, which it probably was. "You're growing up, buddy," Dad said. But Pete did not know if Jayne could be called sexy. She was almost two feet high, all pink with a black bikini painted on and a screw on cap like a hat on the back of her head. He knew Russ would approve, which was the best thing about her. And she was a sign of the funny friendship he and Aunt Helena had. He had written her a thank-you note saying it was his favorite present, but what he truly loved were the new sketchbooks and chalks and charcoals and brushes, all the things he had asked for. His parents had been so careful to get him exactly the right kinds.

Questions

"Tell me something, Pete, buddy," Dad said. They were alone at home because Mom had taken John to his third-grade Valentine's party. "Since we had our talk about sexual intercourse have you had any questions or worries or anything?"

Dad was being serious. There were only a few times a year when he and Pete found themselves uninterrupted in a room together, and usually they stayed quiet with an occasional comment on an article in *Time* or the evening's *Daily News* as they turned the pages across the room from one another.

"I don't have any worries really," Pete said.

"Questions?"

"Not really. I don't need to think about it much yet."

"Your friend Marc acts like it's all he thinks about," Dad said with a snort. He and Mom did not much like

Marc, who unfortunately could be rude. He was over once after school and invited himself to stay for dinner. Mom explained she was serving pork loin and she was concerned because she knew his family was kosher, but Marc said, "Hell, my friggin' parents won't find out." Mom had not known what to say. "Not that religious rules matter to me," she told Pete later, "but it put me in an awkward position." What Dad said now was "That kid is so hopped up all the time."

"It's mostly an act," said Pete.

"He's not your usual sort of friend, Pete. Kids like Russ and Susie are more your style, aren't they?"

"Mom thinks Russ is strange," Pete said. He knew being hopped up was not as bad as being strange and was actually considered cool, while strange was not.

"Russ is still a good egg," Dad said, "and we really do like Susie a lot, buddy."

"So do I," said Pete hoping it would be just enough to please his dad without causing more questions. Dad had asked if Pete had questions or worries, but the worries and questions seemed to be coming more from Dad.

"You and Susie have your artistic side in common. You help inspire each other. I'm fond of Russ and so's your mother, but Susie seems like a grownup already. I know girls grow up quicker than boys, but—"

That was what Mom told Pete too, but it did not seem fair coming from Dad. Time did not move faster for girls. But Pete thought of the eighth-grade cotillion when Susie said "You're a sweet kid" like a college girl in a movie. And then he remembered his terrible embarrassment earlier at the dinner party. He had sat in his hot flannel suit on the black leather seat, and when he got up after dessert Susie had pointed down at the sweat marks his butt had left, two buns with a crack between. Then she stopped her laugh and said, "Oh, I'm sorry, I never should've—forget I even noticed," and then he had to lead her into the ballroom.

"I shouldn't worry about you then, Pete?"

"Nope," Pete said, concentrating on the Milestones column in his magazine.

"We're lucky," Dad said, "to have a son who doesn't make us worry. We're lucky we're not Marc's parents."

Points of the Compass

Sometimes it was awkward having a best friend. You spent most of your free time together but still wanted to do things with other boys. Pete was not good at asking friends over, and it was easier to stick to Russ, who could be snotty about some of their classmates. But Pete's agreeable nature drew others to him anyway. All through junior high and into ninth grade came periods of having a second best friend like Nick at summer camp or Marc. Pete was not surprised when these new friendships led to fooling around. It never did with Nick despite seeing him join the jack-off circle in their cabin, but Marc, who was constantly horny, probably was hanging around with Pete for no other reason. And Wayne, with his jet black hair and eyes and leather jacket with silver snaps, convinced Pete they should practice making out so later they would be good with girls. In ninth grade it was mostly Dirk.

Pete lived in a quiet neighborhood of tall trees and Victorian houses with screen porches in back. One warmish night, Pete and Dirk were lying out in sleeping bags and reading by flashlight. They had to keep quiet because Sarah had her room off the back stairs and her window was right there. They got the giggles over the Junior Anti-Sex League in *1984*. They were already somewhat charged up from listening to Pete's dad's *Noel Coward at Las Vegas* album with the dirty lyrics to "Let's Do It" and then to "It's Too Darn Hot" from *Kiss Me, Kate*.

Then they started wrestling. Dirk was no bigger or stronger than Pete, so neither could pin the other. They kept tumbling about with Pete on top and then Dirk. Pete felt his skin almost boiling, so he pulled off his undershirt and Dirk pulled off his. When they went back to wrestling it felt as if Dirk was boiling too.

Suddenly Sarah's gruff voice came out her window two feet away. "You boys hush up, no more of that messing, I don't want to listen to that stuff." They were silently lying chest to chest in their nest of down sleeping bags. Pete was afraid Sarah knew what he was thinking and that he had a hard-on in his underpants and could feel one in Dirk's. Then Dirk rolled away and said he was tired anyhow.

A week later he invited Pete to his house, which was on the Country Club grounds and seemed huge but not as homey as Pete's or Russ's houses. Mom made snide remarks about the so-called French Provincials and Tudors and Spanish villas at the Country Club with rec rooms and "drapes" and wall to wall carpeting and sliding glass doors and automatic garage openers, for

Christ's sake. Dirk's family had a white maid. She lived over the kitchen wing, but it was far from Dirk's third floor, which was all his.

They went upstairs which had been turned into the deck of an ocean liner with white metal railings hung with life preservers stenciled S. S. *DIRK*. The sloping ceiling was sky blue with a few seagulls, and the low walls were painted with waves and far-off desert islands. There were two doors with fake portholes and brass plates that read "Captain's Quarters" and "Head." Pete knew not to report these details to his mom and give her more to make fun of.

Dirk's room itself had low bunks built into each wall with drawers below them. The dark red floorboards were painted with a large golden compass showing all sixteen points, like East North East and South South West. In one drawer Dirk had stashed the magazines he had found in his brother Hank's closet after he left for college. Those men were not like the Mr. Americas Russ had cut out from comic books for his files. They wore costumes like Greek slaves and ranch hands and warriors from the Amazon, and some wore only bulgy pouches held up by a string.

"Aren't they cool?" Dirk asked. "I have to sneak them back before his Christmas vacation."

Pete and Dirk lay side by side on one bunk and went through page after page without saying anything. Then suddenly they were tumbling off the bunk and rolling across the polished floor. Up there in the Captain's Quarters no one would hear them, no one would come in by mistake.

In Oils

In the fall Dirk's parents sent him to boarding school in the East because his grades were not good enough to get him into Harvard where Hank went. Pete was supposed to go to Yale like his grandfather, but Mom would rather see him at Harvard. Dad had lived at home during the Depression and gone to Northwestern, and cousin Maurice was set for Columbia, so Grandfather said it was up to Pete to go to Yale.

Pete did not miss Dirk. Sometimes he thought about how when they used to wrestle their hard-ons dripped wet through their underpants before they got naked and shot off on each other's stomachs. Otherwise Dirk was boring. Pete thought more often about lying on the beach when Wayne came by and for a while knelt in the sand next to him and he kept looking at the hard muscles in Wayne's thighs. Pete wished they could practice kissing again, but now Wayne was going steady with Peggy.

Everyone assumed Pete was going steady with Susie. Often the two of them stayed late in the art room to work on their oil paintings and talk about teachers and other kids and their families or religion or integration or pacifism. Pete told Susie the scariest thing about being male was that you might have to go into the Army. Susie said the scariest thing about being female was childbirth. Pete told her the way out of the Army was to be 4F but it was considered shameful so he did not plan to resort to it. Susie said that she wanted babies anyway.

She was taller than Pete and angular. She liked to wrap one long skinny arm around him and squeeze his soft shoulders. Once she called him cute as a button, and that became her name for him. Pete could tell that being slender and short and not muscular like Wayne made him more of the friend type. And boys never bothered to start fights with Pete. His drawings got him in good with the cool guys. He had drawn an extremely realistic pencil sketch of one of Wayne's black loafers with drops of red blood seeping out of it that Wayne said was outstanding. Marc asked if he could draw one of a profusely bleeding Cubs cap. Pete had lots of commissions.

But painting in oils for art class was harder. The tones turned murky. Colors built up in layers and kept thickening and muddying. Pete was trying for the soft light of a sunset behind a leafless tree, but the reds and oranges were so heavy. The bare black tree seemed slapped on a solid wall of flame.

"I like how it shimmers behind the branches," Susie said looking over from her easel.

"It's not coming out right," said Pete.

"To my eyes it looks right."

"It's too expressionist. I want to see through the colors even past the horizon."

Susie came and stood behind him with one hand on his shoulder and looked more carefully. "It's hard to do sky, Button. It's like doing glass. My flowers are fine, but my vase is a disaster."

Pete turned on his stool and looked closely at her canvasboard. He said, "I sort of like it that way, it's more of a pot."

"But it's meant to be crystal," said Susie sadly.

For His Private Sketchbook

Pete was surprised to be the first to reach the ridge. He saw before anyone else the vast landscape of countless green mountains and deep valleys and puffs of cloud passing below him, rising, dissipating, and far in the distance the highest snowy peaks of all the Andes.

Here came his new friend Talcott up the stone staircase of the Incas to join him. The other two boys and their Ancient History teacher, whom they now called Jerry, were dawdling below, maybe even resting. "It's a lot cooler up here," panted Talcott. Pete was suddenly aware of everything about him—how sweaty he smelled, the deep breaths he was taking, the way he swung his long arms to cool himself off. They looked almost alike in their leather hiking boots with leather laces, their baggy dusty chinos and white T-shirts wet in the armpits. They were only reconnoitering for the big trek tomorrow, so they had left their identical fifty-pound rucksacks down in camp. "What a kick, man," Talcott said. He grabbed Pete's soft bicep and squeezed it in his excitement.

Sharing a pup tent, farting from the odd things they ate and drank, sleeping beside each other in their down bags, then waking in the dewy mornings and looking over at Talcott resting his brown head resting on his light-brown arm, Pete did not know how he could still keep what he felt inside him, but he knew he had to. He did say, philosophically, "Being way up here makes me somehow love the whole world."

"Man," Talcott whispered, then he shouted, "Yeah, I love even you!" and leaned his head over to smack a brief exuberant kiss on Pete's sweaty cheek.

"You're such a weirdo," Pete said as he was expected to when Talcott went into his beatnik act, but Pete's heart was shaking in his chest. This was the Talcott he had surreptitiously watched from across the classroom and down his row of first basses in chorus but never talked to. Then Talcott's parents, who seemed to know Pete's parents, had convinced them to sign Pete up for this amazing trip. Mom and Dad told him they thought it would help get him over his timidity and of course would be good for his art. And in the spring they suggested he bring Talcott out to Gramma's so they could get to know each other better before Peru. There the two of them had driven the tractor up the rutted road and all around the meadow, Talcott steering wildly on purpose and Pete standing on the hitch behind with his hands on Talcott's waist to keep steady. The sensation had lasted for days in Pete's hands. He had drawn the scene many times in his private sketchbook. Now he would be drawing this scene too, a couple of high school boys way above clouds on these crumbling overgrown stone steps over five hundred years old. Pete had been lifted out of flat suburban Illinois to this Peruvian mountaintop and been kissed on the cheek by someone completely unlike himself in every way.

In the Ruins

In the ruins of Machu Picchu, lying under the stars in their sleeping bags, Pete and Talcott had been talking in soft voices, heads inches apart. The others had camped on a lower terrace, but not being sleepy yet Pete and Talcott had climbed higher up. Talcott said it was too cool a thing to be in such a place at night and sleep through it. The next day they would be leaving over the mountain on the unmapped Inca road carrying what they needed on their backs like explorers.

For a while Talcott explained Zen Buddhism to Pete, and then he got talking about the blues versus rhythm and blues. Then he wanted Pete to define cubism and Dada and abstract expressionism. Talcott said what had come to matter most to him in life was being able to express things completely at the moment he felt them. That was Zen, that was blues, that was modern painting too, wasn't it? So Pete softly touched the back of Talcott's hand resting there in the stubbly grass of the terrace and said, "I guess then I meant to say up on the mountain that I loved you too."

Talcott's hand jumped away. "In the cosmic sense like we were saying. You said you loved the whole world."

"Then you said you loved even me."

"Yeah, and then you said I was such a weirdo." He was looking at Pete's hand still there in the starlight unable to draw itself back. "But I didn't mean I wanted us to make out, man," Talcott said.

"I didn't say anything about making out," Pete said but knew he had already shown it in the way he had touched the cold skin of Talcott's hand. Now Talcott was looking at his face with penetrating eyes lit by the stars. "I didn't mean I wanted to make out," Pete said again. Talcott turned and looked blankly up at the sky. He made a frustrated sound with his lips.

All afternoon Pete had been imagining kissing him tonight. He and Dirk sometimes kissed when they wrestled. He and Marc even kissed a few times during their beat-off sessions. With Wayne it had been only kissing along with feeling each other up. But Talcott seemed older than any of them, not because he was already sixteen but because, even though he acted like a beatnik, he did not ever act like a kid. Pete turned on his side to stare into the wall of stones rising beside them to the topmost terrace.

"Hey, man," Talcott said, "we don't have to get into this." He put his hand on Pete's shoulder and pulled him back so now Pete was also staring up at the stars and the sky in its blackness. "We both know it's normal to have homosexual feelings, they're part of the stage we're at, but we don't have to act on them. I bet what you really feel, Pete, is homesick," he added in a calmer voice.

"Maybe I just love you as a person," Pete said quietly.

"I love you as a person too," Talcott said. "Now let's get to sleep."

Pete thought for a while. They had a long trek ahead up over the mountain and beyond the ridge they had climbed that afternoon and down across the knife edge, as Jerry called it, into those dry green forests. They would have to hack their way through the vines and creepers looking for the half buried stones of the ancient road. They would go as far as their oatmeal cakes and dried fruit would take them.

Now Pete was remembering the night on the bus when the Indian ladies in the seat opposite had taken up a song to pass the slow time on the high dark plain before descending to the lights of Cuzco. Peruvian music had a strange quality. In market places it bounced along strumming and tootling, but to Pete's ear the tunes were nonetheless sad. When those ladies with their long skirts and bowler hats had sung without the happy instruments to keep them going their melodies hung mournfully in Pete's ears along with the fussy clucking of a hen on the overhead rack and the worried snuffling of a piglet amid the sacks piled in the aisle.

On the Inca Road

On the ashen mountain, lost, where there was no map, no human footprint, Pete was not afraid. The other boys were. That morning they had taken a ridge that ran not above the Urubamba Valley as they thought but further off into the unknown. The intermittent steps of the Inca Road had misled them. And then leaning out to cut a sapling to replace his lost canteen cap Jerry had slipped down the slope and sprained an ankle. He was still hobbling. And smoke was rising up from smouldering fires, spontaneous combustion burning off a mountainside of dry undergrowth. The five of them were safely above those creeping little flames, but the summit loomed over them with daylight fading behind it fast.

Jerry said they needed to gain the next ridge and follow it down to the river. He said his ankle was fine. Ed and Farley were complaining at every step, and Talcott had joined them now and left Pete to his silent slogging. Ed's whimpers and Talcott's cusses floated down to slower Pete, who felt inwardly stronger than they were. It was a matter of lifting one foot and then the other and not complaining.

When they gained the ridge the going got easier and sunnier. They stopped to eat their last oatmeal cakes and drain their canteens. They had one hour of light to make it down. But the ridge descended too sharply and came to an abrupt precipice. With not enough time to climb back up they made camp on a rocky shelf ten feet wide as darkness came on.

No one was talking now. They lined their sleeping bags perpendicular to the edge, and Pete lay next to Talcott for the first time since their midnight talk in the ruins. He soon heard the steady breathing of Talcott's exhausted sleep. It was suddenly very cold.

Why was Pete not afraid? He had thought about it and knew for sure he was not. He had been scared the first day on the knife edge, but that was because the bright void on either side had dazzled him. Now he was on a sturdy ledge with darkness all around and no stars because it was beginning to spit a freezing rain. Farley was sniffling on the other side of Talcott.

Pete knew he would get home to Illinois or at least was not imagining otherwise. What he was afraid of in his life had turned out to be that he still wanted to touch Talcott lying there beside him and that Talcott was not even in the deepest corner of his brain thinking of Pete now but probably dreaming of girls.

Retirement

When he came safely home, Pete spent the last weeks of summer at Gramma's place with Mom and John, who was ten and got easily bored. Pete had all his art supplies, and when the weather was dry he would take himself to a quiet spot on the property to paint and sketch. When it rained or was too hot he would work inside on paintings inspired by his Peruvian sketchbook. There were walls of great stones irregularly cut but perfectly fit into each other. There was the Hitching Post of the Sun from every angle. There was a ragged line of mountains, a beggar woman with her children on the night cold street in Cuzco, a bell tower of a colonial church, a reed boat on Lake Titicaca. But Pete's impressions had begun to fade, for now an Andean tree tangled in creepers gave way under his brush to an Illinois black walnut in a gulch by a field.

One sticky August day, still trying to hold onto Peru, Pete had sat at Gramma's sewing table while she rocked and darned socks and he traced again and again the stones of Ollantaytambo. Gramma's FM announced Bartok's *Second Quartet*, and some gloomy music began. Pete did not understand why Gramma appreciated something so hard to hear the beauty in, but she had grown up with the modern composers. "They're my generation," she told Pete.

He and Gramma did not talk much when they were alone together. If Mom and John were there they would break the spell, but they had gone into town to entertain John with a barge trip and some ice cream.

When the quartet struck a painful harmony Pete looked toward Gramma to see what her expression might be. It was reposeful, her fingers picking away with the darning needle, her eyes fixed calmly on her work. The thin line of her lips was neither a smile nor a frown. Concentration, Pete thought. This life up above the river is how a life should always be. As he retraced the strangely shaped stones he wondered if he would ever be as lucky.

His Three Selves

"Mom?" Pete said quietly so as not to wake her but to see if she might still be awake.

She turned over on the couch where she had been waiting up for him and said softly, "You're in late." Dad always went to bed at ten, but Mom never felt safe until Pete got home.

"It's after midnight," he admitted. "I meant to be here sooner, but Heath and I went to see *La Strada* a second time and then hung out at his house and I didn't realize."

He would have dropped Heath off and driven straight home but got persuaded to park in the alley and sneak into the store room above the garage without Heath's parents hearing them. Then they fucked on the old couch up there. Pete was used to it now and truly liked it. Heath kept an old towel and some Vaseline hidden under the couch.

It felt odd to come home and talk to Mom right afterwards, not that she suspected. Heath was even more of an intellectual than Russ, who did not like him, but Mom preferred Heath because he was not such an odd-ball. He seemed the most normal nice smart kid in Pete's class.

Mom sat up and pulled her floppy flannel robe up around her neck and patted the couch next to her for Pete to sit down.

"I love that movie," he said. "I love black and white, you can see the edges of every shape. You catch the contrasts and how they fit together, the composition. It's not the same in color."

"Foreigners make the good movies," Mom said. She lay her pink flannel sleeve on the back of Pete's plaid shirt and clutched his waist with her warm hand. "It's nice you've got friends you do such interesting things with. You've always been lucky with friends, Russ and Susie and what was his name—Dirk, well, he was rather dull—and good old Talcott." She let out a bemused sigh. "When I think of you in that photo leading the way with your machete—that was my little Pete!"

An hour before when he was with Heath he had been an entirely different person from the son sitting beside his mom chatting the way they always did. And at the movies he had been yet someone else, his eyes filled with ideas to discuss on the drive home. Pete liked all three of his selves and did not want to part with any of them.

Ancient History

There was a fierce summer storm with loud thunder and buckets of rain. Heath and Pete had snuck out at midnight and met on a corner to go running in their gym shorts and sneakers the half mile to the Country Club. Lightning was flashing across the golf course. They passed Dirk's house, all dark except for the portico lamp, and kept running onto a fairway. At the sixth green they took off their squishy sneakers and left them upside down where they could find them later by the flag. Heath was trying to make Pete get more exercise.

They began running again, into the rough then through a strip of woods where they first took off their gym shorts and then also their jocks and, wet all over, jumped in and out of the trees, dodging for cover when the lightning came. In darkness they made it across another fairway to a small clump of bushes. They were running like the messengers they had read about in Ancient History. Pete clenched his fists as if they held something he must not lose.

Here came Heath leaping long-legged across a sand trap kicking up wet sand with bare feet and then flinging himself on the sodden grass of a green. "9" read the flapping wet flag when the lightning flashed. Pete began running toward him, then Heath was up again, and Pete ran after him. He had never run so hard.

There were no lights in any of the houses on the far edges of the golf course, only distant hazy streetlights behind the shadows of trees. Pete hoped Heath remembered where they had left their shorts.

Later when they were creeping up the rickety stairs to the store room over Heath's garage Pete asked, "What would happen if we got caught up here?"

"They never check on me. My mother would think we were wrestling."

It was dusty and spidery and damp, the windowpanes were cracked and sooty in the streetlamp light, the overstuffed couch smelled moldy, and there was a trail of mouse turds along one cushion. Heath brushed them off, sat down, and pulled wet Pete down next to him by the waistband.

"Why would we be wrestling with our clothes off?"

"My mother thinks men are a different species. She doesn't try to understand. Anyway she's not your mother, so what's your problem?"

Heath had used the grimy towel to dry himself off. He pulled at Pete's gym shorts again so he could reach into his jockstrap and get things started.

60

Thanks a Pile

Russ was sitting on Pete's back porch on the creaky wicker couch across from Pete in the creaky wicker chair. A melancholy summer rain was filling in the screen's tiny squares with a film of water. Pete had not spent much time with Russ the past year, and now they would be going off to college. Though Russ had been all obsessed with Samantha it was still Pete's fault they had drifted apart.

"I concede I'm not Ivy League material," Russ said with an edgy sigh.

"Don't be stupid."

"I've always been self-motivated," Russ explained, "just not in the direction of the assignments."

"The stupid assignments are way beneath you, that's why."

"I'll be happier at a state school. You're going to be so lost, Dabney." Russ gave Pete a severe stare and narrowed it to a meaner squint. Pete knew it was another dose of his ongoing punishment for getting into Yale because of his grandfather and Harvard, where his parents convinced him to go. Then Russ changed the subject. "This rain—" he said, "it's how I feel about Samantha. Drippy."

"I bet at Rutgers you'll find some girl who'll like you back for once," Pete said trying to be kindlier than Russ.

"Pete, I wonder if you'll find anyone at Harvard at all, female or otherwise," Russ said, not nastily now but as if he truly was puzzled. "You never talk about love or lust or even wanting a date. I suppose it all goes into your art. That's what Susie says. It'd be sort of cool, wouldn't it, if you turned out to be a secret homo?"

"Cool?"

"Or maybe even one of those fetishists in *The Psychology of Sex* with the boots and the riding crops."

"Thanks a pile," said Pete worried that Sarah in the kitchen might be listening.

Russ lifted his arm from the back of the wicker couch and ran his fingers along the wet screen. "Kidding," he said. Pete shook his head at him but could not think of what to say next. It was a subject he almost wished they could keep talking about. But Russ was going on. "Well, what I wrote her was 'Dearest Sammy, You must be relieved I'll soon be out of your life.' Does that sound like self pity? I wanted to write her an honest letter. I know she hates my moping."

"There'll be someone new at college," Pete assured him. "Girls won't know what you were like in high school."

"Thanks a pile," said Russ. "I'll be an entirely new person? I'll be suddenly cool?"

Pete tried to look at Russ as if he had never seen him before but could not imagine being attracted to him. He could not figure out what it was that was missing.

Polite Conversation

Pete knew that Dirk's brother Hank had gone on to Harvard Law. He sent him a note, then got a note back, and eventually reached him by phone and explained he was a Harvard freshman who knew his brother. He was hoping they could meet at Albiani's cafeteria across Harvard Square from his dorm. What he was really hoping was that Hank still liked those kinds of magazines Dirk had found in his closet. He hoped Hank might bring up the subject of bodybuilding and things like that.

When they sat down with their trays of English muffins and tea Hank mostly talked about what a bitch law school was and made it clear he was very busy all the time. He did not even particularly look at Pete. But Pete felt strangely bold. "You're like a more serious grown-up version of the way I remember Dirk," he said.

"That's why I'm here and Dirk's not," Hank said. He was pulling his arms out of his sport coat. His short-sleeve shirt showed he had not lost his immense biceps.

Pete decided to try one more time. "You still do your weightlifting?"

"You boys were so creepy about that," Hank said. "I never had any privacy with you two little pansies in the house."

Pete could not tell if he was meant to laugh at that, but he did. Hank kept looking around Albiani's to see if he knew anyone. Then Pete heard more about law school and finally Hank did ask what courses he was taking without paying much attention to the answer. It was like talking to Pete's roommate Tom. They tolerated each other for the times they were together but went out to their separate lives, which for Pete seemed to mean tagging along with one group or another or sitting down with a lonely African student in the Freshman Union and making polite conversation.

"You doing any sport?" Hank asked and then answered himself, "No, I don't suppose you are."

"Required swimming," Pete said.

"Yeah, all those naked little undergrads," said Hank.

It worried Pete how they were not allowed swim-suits. They had to practice life-saving carries and mouth-to-mouth resuscitation in the nude. A few professors were usually sitting fully clothed in the bleachers watching but luckily no professor of his.

"So I'll tell Dirk I heard from you," Hank said slinging his sport coat over his shoulder and picking up his tray with one strong hand. "He loves his crappy college. Already got himself a girlfriend."

Pete was looking at Hank's flexed arm muscles. "Do you have a girlfriend?" he asked casually as Hank was about to turn away.

"Do you think in law school I'd have time for a girlfriend?"

Pete shrugged then gave an offhand farewell wave and opened his paperback of *Pride and Prejudice*. He took another small sip of his now lukewarm tea.

The Renaissance

Pete enjoyed Gen Ed and Humanities, did all right in French, and squeaked by in Geology, but his art history course was what mattered to him most. He had not realized Fine Arts was a separate subject you could concentrate in. That nearly made it worth being away from home and having to study so hard.

He got a sexy letter from Heath at Princeton. "Everything one hears about the Princeton Belly Rub is true," it said. "The jocky preps have to get shit-faced first but the choirboy types only need one beer. There's some pretty boys down here." Then he went into a description of how he fucked a prep named Ethan who played lacrosse.

Pete had nothing to write back except that he envied Heath and that it was not like that up here. It probably was, but Pete did not know how to go about it. When there was a beer party in his dorm he went to the movies with Olokongwu, and when they came home there was beer and puke dripping down the staircase and guys passed out in the halls.

Pete had begun to think about art differently. The more he studied the less he dared do his own. He did some sketching when Tom was at class but kept the sketchbook in a locked desk drawer. Sometimes he drew impressions of boys swimming or imaginings of the jocks next door who played their records loud and yelled something once about doing the Homosexual Twist. Pete sent a few to Heath, who took a long time writing back and never mentioned them. After that Pete did not write again. It felt as if their friendship was disappearing. They would not even see each other at Christmas because Heath was going to Aspen with his family to ski.

When they at last got through the Renaissance in his art history survey Pete began to relax some about his own work. He set up his easel by his window and painted what he saw across the Square. Tom complained about the paint smell, so he closed the door between their two rooms. Instead of having a living room and shared bedroom like everyone else they had split their double though it meant Pete had to go through Tom's room to get to his. Luckily Mac and Don across the hall had asked him to apply with them for a triple next year. Pete had begun to have his own friends.

From the Artist's Angle

Aunt Helena had invited Pete for a theater weekend over spring vacation. With Maurice living up at Columbia she had moved to a studio building on Fourth Avenue. Not that she was an artist but she liked living among artists. That was one reason, Pete knew, why she loved him so much.

His cousin came down to let him in, and they rode up together in a freight elevator. He told Pete his rucksack made him look like a hick. Maurice had always been snobbish about being from New York City as opposed to Chicago.

Aunt Helena's door was open at the end of a long corridor. She was stretching out her arms and calling, "Honey! Darling! College boy!" She hugged Pete tightly three separate times before letting him inside then pointed over her shoulder at the door across the hall and whispered, "My neighbors design bathing suits for fairies. Ain't that the nertz?"

Maurice tossed the rucksack into the loft above a row of closets.

"That's your room up there, sweetie," Aunt Helena said, "if you don't mind a top bunk. We've got all sorts of tickets. Tonight *A Funny Thing* with Zero Mostel, tomorrow *Too True to Be Good* by George Bernard Shaw—fabulous cast: Lillian Gish, Cedric Hardwicke, Cyril Ritchard, Robert Preston, Glynis Johns—and then Sunday *The Blacks* at St. Mark's. I'm too excited!"

Pete was glad he had worn a coat and tie and his dress shoes even if his shirt and corduroys were rumpled from napping on the bus.

"The Shaw is brilliant," said Maurice. "I'm not sure Pete is ready for Genet though, Mom."

"Maurice is only stopping by to say hello, sweetie. He has a date tonight, so we won't have to listen to his opinions. I'm sure Pete's ready for everything. This is New York! We're taking a cab uptown for dinner near the Alvin, honey. And tomorrow the Museum of Modern Art. You'll explain it all to me from the artist's angle."

Aunt Helena was grayer and more wrinkled than when she came out to help Grandmother after Grandfather's death, but she had her dangling silver earrings on and one of her bright scarves from India wrapped about her neck and dark nail polish, fingers and toes, and tiny high heel shoes with almost no shoe, only straps.

"We'll have to speed out, darling," she said. "Maurice will grab us a cab. I could never get Paul and

Rachel to come for a real theater weekend. They're too Midwestern. I used to blame your mother and her farmy summer place, but I think my brother's the real stick in the mud."

Pete smiled as he tightened his tie.

"Don't you look swank," Aunt Helena said. She grabbed her little handbag and checked for the tickets. Maurice was holding up her fur coat. Pete realized because of his late bus he had only made it just in time. Aunt Helena had been nervously waiting for him, worried the weekend would not work out as perfectly as she had planned.

Keep-Away

The boys playing keep-away across the river reminded Pete of years ago in Grandfather's back yard when Maurice had tossed him a football so suddenly he did not see it coming. Grandfather had driven up the drive in his new Lincoln, and Maurice told him what a spaz Pete was. But later Grandfather presented Pete with his old Yale helmet. It was of soft worn brown leather and painted on top with blue and white stripes. Pete loved how it looked and felt on his head. Sometimes he wore it when he studied to help him concentrate. He kept it on the shelf in his room at home.

It had surprised him to find that at college even football players were interested in art and history and famous novels. It was probably the same at Yale because at this age everyone was expected to like his studies. No one here would kid Pete for coming down to the river to read. Other students were sitting or lying on the grass with books. It was a sunny day before finals.

Pete decided it was hot enough to take off his plaid shirt, spread it on the soft grass, and lie on his back in the sun. Others had. It felt wonderful, the sun on his skin for the first time in months, but also something else. If someone walked by and looked at him or stopped to talk then something might occur without his having caused it. He could be simply a boy. He could lean his head back in the grass and look into the sharp blue sky and stop being a particular Pete Dabney. No one could tell how aware he was of his bare chest in the sunlight or how little he felt like those boys tossing around the fluorescent orange rubber football. He closed his eyes and let the minutes pass.

"Getting some sun?"

He blinked then pulled himself up on his elbows and looked closer. Probably a grad student—polo shirt, slacks, lots of curly brown hair. "Yes," he said stupidly.

The grad student sat down and pulled his knees to his chest and hugged onto them. "Great day," he said. "I should be studying."

"So should I," said Pete.

"*From David to Delacroix.*" The grad student was pointing to Pete's book having pronounced "David" the American way and "croix" as "croy."

"For Fine Arts."

"My name happens to be David," the grad student said.

"Mine's Pete." He could tell if they shook hands it would put this meeting on the wrong track, so he let his hands lie in the grass. Enough silence followed to insure this was not the usual college conversation.

After a bit David said softly, "You're the color of honey."

"Oh?" said Pete as blankly as he could.

"Lickable," said David.

"Are you a grad student?" Pete asked to slow it down.

"So you can tell. Hey, don't be shy."

"I'm not," Pete said though he would truly have been shy in any normal circumstance. In this one, he realized, his appearing to be shy was what David liked and after saying he was not shy he had to keep pretending he was.

David had just touched his arm. "Soft," he murmured.

They did not say anything while Pete concentrated on feeling the warm sun on his skin and David kept staring at his nipples.

"I'm a tutor. You're definitely not taking any Economics. We would've noticed you before."

"I'm a freshman," Pete said.

"Ah," said David. He was gently rubbing Pete's arm, which caused Pete to assent with a quick nod when David said, "Want to come back to my room?"

Pete sat up and buttoned his shirt around him but did not tuck it in. It was good not to have to say anything more. He accompanied this David across Memorial Drive, and eventually they turned silently into an unfamiliar stairwell in one of the houses then slipped behind an unknown door. "Hush," David said though Pete had not said anything. He began unbuttoning Pete's shirt and kissing each revealed bit of skin as if he had not seen it minutes before out in the sun.

Great Art

They were all together at Gramma's for the whole month of August though Dad had to go back to Chicago for a few days in the middle. John was not as bored because he had his friend Keith there, and Mom and Gramma made big farm meals with corn on the cob and fresh tomato and cucumber salads and played canasta with John and Keith every evening. Pete had never liked card games. He did not have the competitive spirit. What had kept him going his first year of college was wanting his parents to see him as a good student.

He was working on a portrait of the '53 DeSoto staring out of the garage beside the '42 Chrysler Gramma had refused to trade in. Lemuel kept them both in good running order. Pete had not thought about cars for a long time. Even the DeSoto looked old now.

Exclamations from the canasta players floated out from the porch. Pete was trying to capture the setting sunlight on the cars' grilles. Then he sensed Lemuel standing silently behind him. "That's a darn good painting, Pete," he said. "Your gramma told me how good you got. I see how it got you into that college."

"It didn't though. Unfortunately it's not an art school."

"That shows what I know," Lemuel said. He stood there awhile longer. It made Pete think of the times he himself used to stand around watching Lemuel tune up the Chrysler. Then Lemuel said, "Hey, I'd like you to do one for me sometime. I mean of me. To send to my sister in South Dakota. I ask you as a favor, Pete, because I sure can't pay for great art!"

Pete had not been up in Lemuel's room above the garage in some years. When he saw it the next afternoon it looked exactly the way he remembered it.

"I'll set here on my chair by the window, and you set there on the bed and draw me so I come out looking handsomer than I am." He gave Pete a wink then added, "So my sister will want to frame it on her wall."

For a time Pete had to look very closely at the way Lemuel's long body sat stiffly on the old chair and at how his gnarly hands held onto each other. Eventually his own hand began moving across the paper. But it was going to be difficult.

As he sketched first in charcoal and then tried some color, then sketched some more, he began to see the Lemuel he remembered as clearly as the Lemuel in front of him. He knew he would have to draw how his jeans tightened up at the crotch from the way he sat. Pete could still picture what was in there. Lemuel was almost fifty, but Pete did not have to change him to make him more handsome. He could paint him exactly as he saw him.

Do You Remember?

"Do you remember, buddy, when you sent your drawing of Mom's yellow convertible to the *Lois and Louie* show and they showed it on TV?"

"You were six," Mom said.

"When I was six," said John, "a little kid could never get something on TV, it was all network by then. Can you pass the butter?"

"Remember *Breezy, Don and Vera*?" asked Pete.

"Another dorky local show," John told Keith.

"Mom, you claimed they were trying to cash in on *Kukla, Fran and Ollie*. You were always disillusioning me. I preferred *Breezy, Don and Vera*."

"You would," said John salting his buttery cob of corn.

"I remember Vera, but who was Don? Breezy was a raccoon."

Dad was also feeling nostalgic tonight. "And do you remember the first time you drew a Nash, Pete? And then the catalog of cars you made for my birthday— what, thirty-fifth? I hope your mother still has them tucked away somewhere."

"I have every drawing you ever sent me," Gramma said.

"And I have John's cardboard poop family too," said Mom.

"Thanks for mentioning it, Mom," John said snidely. Keith was looking quizzical, but John made the cut-off sign across his own throat.

"Oh, I know all about them," Gramma said. "I took Gramma Poop as a compliment. You were an odd little boy, John."

"Unlike Pete," John said. "No, Pete was never odd. He was always taken seriously, weren't you, Pete? How did he pull it off?" he asked Keith who also had an older brother.

Dad was rotating his ear of corn in front of his mouth. He never went down the rows but chewed round and round the cob the way all the Dabneys did from stalk to tip. "One other thing, Pete," he said, "do you remember when I took you and your cousin Maurice to the Cubs game and you insisted I buy you a Phillies cap instead?"

"Somehow that doesn't surprise me," said John, then, "Dad, why don't you ask me if I remember anything?"

Dad thought a second and said, "I guess because it doesn't seem as long ago."

Wednesdays at Four

"Thanks as always," said Pete, getting back into his clothes.

"You don't have to say thanks. I could as well be thanking you, but it's a fair exchange."

"I suppose," said Pete. The aftermath was the awkward part. It was easy when he came up the stairwell and tapped on David's door because he was excited and expectant and nothing else mattered.

"We each give the other what he wants, so it works."

"Definitely," Pete said with his eyes on his feet as he pulled up his wool socks. He was probably blushing but knew David liked that. David was still naked, lying beside him on the bed. After sex David always rolled off him onto his back so Pete could drape his arm around his hairy chest and rest his cheek there. They would lie together for the usual ten minutes then Pete would sit up.

The pink baby lotion bottle stood on the bedside table with pink drips smeared on its sides. There was a pile of messy Kleenex and David's garnet ring, which he took off to avoid scratching Pete. David was good at playing rough without ever actually hurting. It was so much better than with Heath when neither of them really knew what he was doing. Pete hoped sex would keep getting better as he grew older. It was not something kids naturally knew how to do well.

Now David was stroking the back of the sweater Pete had pulled over his head. His touch was gentle, unerotic, meant to relax him, but it made him think David was affectionately letting him know it was over for today. "When do you want to come by again?"

"This time is still good. Next week?" Pete asked.

"The boys in my entry must assume it's your tutorial," David said then suddenly grabbed Pete tight at the waist and pulled him down against his naked body and gave him a deep kiss. "I can't help doing that," he said. Pete blushed again. "You mind?"

He shook his head. He was shy now, but he had been completely unshy half an hour ago with David tumbling him around and whispering crazy things in his ear. Pete did not know how to act together except when both of them were naked.

He put on his boots and parka and knit hat and mittens and walked to the door beside David, who had wrapped a skimpy linen-service towel barely around his waist and stayed behind the door when he opened it. "I was afraid the snow would've kept you away today, Pete."

"Oh, never," said Pete cheerily on his way down the stairs.

Macedonia

Mac and Don called their triple "Macedonia," which did not account for Pete. Pete got a bottom bunk, and Mac and Don switched off semesters getting the solo bedroom. They filled the living room with three big armchairs from Goodwill and in the winter made fires in the fireplace and all sat reading as if it was their private men's club. Don was a Classics major and had a whole story going about being Macedonians and how Pete was a dark wavy-haired Persian boy they brought back from the wars. Mac was taking Social Relations and getting political. He and Don were Easterners but from regular public schools. Don was Catholic and had a slight Boston accent he was getting rid of. Mac was from the Philadelphia suburbs. He was willowy in an almost feminine way that Pete found reassuring. Don was a rower and liked to grapple with Mac and sometimes with Pete in a considerately underpowered fashion. They had lots of dates who always sided with Pete when Mac and Don ribbed him for being a wonk or for refusing to try pot. Pete's steadiness helped them appear irresponsible, which girls seemed to like, and he made a good audience for their shenanigans.

He often drew them sitting around their suite. Mac was pleased with his scruffy new radical image, and when Don made crew he offered his musculature to Pete for anatomical studies though he always kept his shorts on. Being "Persian Pete" was sort of fun, but they never played the game outside their suite or in front of Mac's and Don's dates. Pete realized being roommates was a special thing somewhere between being brothers and being friends. He managed to suppress the romantic fantasies they had once stirred up in him. The main thing was, despite their joking, they took him seriously. Don said he was in awe of Pete's art. They were rough soldiers in the army of Alexander the Great, and he was an aesthetic *ephebos* from the exotic East—they meant the Midwest—who found safety in their company. Sitting in their chairs before the fire Pete realized they both loved him in their funny way, maybe even were in love with him, the way they were in love with politics and crew and each other, and their studies, and with girls and all of young life. Sometimes they reminded him of Talcott.

The Space Program

When he was home for spring vacation Mom had him and John go with her to visit Sarah, who had settled into her church home where she was much happier. She did not have to climb stairs or run herd on John anymore.

For Pete Chicago now meant his hours spent at the Art Institute or the time he wandered around on his own and found under the El tracks near Wacker Drive a newsstand with issues of *Adonis* and *Physique Pictorial* hanging in plain sight. He was too timid to buy one though it made his heart race to see them clipped there on the rack.

Now Mom drove them way beyond the Loop in the '64 Dart Pete felt no attachment to. It had been some years since he cared about the new models. On a wide empty boulevard of dark red brick houses, which Mom said used to be mansions of the wealthy, she pulled up at one with an ugly one story yellow brick addition. The main building had a faded sign over the carved oak door that read TABERNACLE HOUSE, but Mom led Pete and John to the plate glass door in the new wing. There came Sarah shuffling along in pale green slippers on the gray linoleum.

When they took seats in the room she shared with an older, fatter lady named Bessie she poured out what she called "a spot of tea" for each and opened the box of caramels Mom had brought.

"They're for you and Bessie," Mom said.

"They're likely all for Bessie," grumped Sarah, passing Pete the box. He took one, and so did John.

When offered the box Bessie said, "No, I thank you," and sat quietly listening to her roommate brag about her two nice young men.

Pete could see how forgetful she was getting when she asked, "You got any colored boys with you down there at Yale, Pete?"

He did not correct her about Harvard but said yes there were quite a few and he even had an African friend named Olokongwu. He thought of telling her how his roommate Mac collected money for the Student Nonviolent Coordinating Committee but did not know what she as a Republican made of all that.

"Mr. Dabney used to tell me they had colored boys at Yale now."

"Ain't that something!" said Bessie.

"Pete and John have no prejudice," Sarah said. "I taught them the way I did Helena and Paul." Mom seemed pleased her sons were letting themselves be shown off. She was not going to butt in and take over the conversation. She was sitting back and listening.

Now Sarah was going on about the Space Program. She said it was all foolishness. God would never let anybody touch his moon. Pete knew he would feel bad when they had to go because he might never see her again.

Fourth Floor

There was a bathroom on each of the undergraduate library's five levels. The second and fourth floors had smaller, less busy ones with only three stalls. The sound of the outer door gave warning before anyone opened the inner door. What went on behind the stall doors could stop until the newcomer had either left or lingered. Then they could resume the toe tapping and note passing and peeking through the holes bored in the marble dividers at lap level.

Once a long quiet stretch with Pete in one stall and someone unknown in another had led to a cautious unlatching of both stall doors. Still seated, with corduroys at his ankles, Pete had opened his door enough to see a tall boy in unzipped jeans standing there. He let him slip in. "If anyone comes I'll stand up on the seat," the boy whispered.

No one came. Pete was nervous, but the boy who said his name was Jeremy had two roommates and so did Pete so there was nowhere else to go. They tried different positions but having their pants around their ankles made it awkward. Still Pete kept hoping they might meet up again. Sometimes instead of studying he would sit alone in that fourth floor bathroom and wait. If he tried to read a book his mind would wander, so he just sat. Mostly he felt stupid and depressed when he had wasted a sunny afternoon like that, but the chance of hearing someone enter the next stall and sit down and also wait kept Pete coming back.

There were things written on the insides of the stall doors by ballpoint pens pressing hard into the wood. This is also part of my education, Pete thought. He had similar feelings when he dared to go to the bar in Boston David had told him about. He had stood in a dark corner with a Coke and thought how even if he spoke to no one he was safe in a secret world where men had the same yearnings he did.

But the bathroom was even safer because you could only get glimpses through the little holes or under the marble dividers, and only when the scrawled notes got you very excited might you risk following someone out hoping he would not change his mind when he saw you and disappear into the stacks, hoping he might have a place you could both go.

Cool Deal

John flew out to visit the fall of Pete's senior year. He was mildly appreciative of the old brick buildings and the courtyards and of Pete's living room with the fireplace and armchairs, but what impressed him most was everyone's long hair. John said his own crewcut made him feel stupid. He told Pete he would never again let Mom send him to the barber. Pete's hair only curled over his ears and flopped onto his eyebrows, but Don had grown his frizzy hair to look like a Brillo pad and Mac had enough long hair in back to tie into a ponytail. John had not realized Pete had such extremely cool friends.

Pete did not expect his brother to apply to Harvard though Mom and Dad clearly hoped he might return not quite so set on Wisconsin. Pete liked how John never wanted to follow his example. He was the scientific one and had his own ideas.

Don had nicely taken him over to see the bio labs so Pete could do his Ingres paper, but then Mac came out of the solo room, draped himself over the sagging green armchair, and said, "Don says we're taking little brother to our party tonight. Is that cool?"

Pete said, "Sure," knowing it would make John's visit.

"Naturally the girls want us to drag you too. It'll be kind of lively. Music and dope. Is John a virgin?" Mac asked staring with his aqueous pale eyes.

"I assume. I don't know for sure."

"Well, what would you know, buttfucker?" Mac said.

It was one of their routines. Pete came back with, "Well, what would you know, muffdiver?"

"Well, what would you know, horsedick?" said Mac giving up quickly and going back into his room.

When John returned he slouched into the ripped gray corduroy armchair tapping his foot and pinching at his short brown hair. "So what about this party?" he said.

Pete watched his nervous eyes. He reminded himself that John was only sixteen and had never been east and might even still be a virgin. "I'll come too," Pete said.

"Cool deal," said John as if it did not matter. He and his friends pretended they had already done everything there was to be done while Pete pretended he had never done anything at all.

A Possibility

When Pete dropped by at Christmas he found Heath had acquired an additional layer of sophistication. He told Pete he was lovers with his History professor and mostly living with him in his house. They went into New York to restaurants, plays, and the opera, and even Heath's parents knew. "They've adjusted," he told Pete. There was now no question of sneaking off to the store room above the garage though after all these years Pete still wished they could.

When he met with Susie they had a long talk about her new boyfriend, a grad student who was getting pretty serious, and then it was Pete's turn but he had nothing to report. "Haven't you figured out who you really are yet, Button? I mean it was so important to me back when," she said, "to have you as my ostensible boyfriend, but I've always wondered if you might really want to be more with a man. I could even see it in the way you used to draw boys. I'm not criticizing. I understand because I feel that way about boys too."

"It's a possibility," Pete said. The cold wind as they walked along the lake kept him from having to say much.

"I shouldn't psychoanalyze you," Susie said.

He heard cold sand crunching under his shoes. "Is it something you have to think about or doesn't it just happen?" he asked.

"Probably the latter," Susie said. "Maybe someone will come along and you'll finally know."

Later he saw Russ who had had two girlfriends by now and was planning on going to law school.

And here was Pete still occasionally visiting David, passing by that Jeremy in the Yard as if they did not recognize each other, or taking the M.T.A. over to Charles Street where if he looked back at men and they looked back at him they might both stare into shop windows until the man would say "I have a place" and Pete would nod and follow him. He had met a carpenter who took him up Beacon Hill to the apartment he was renovating. He met a businessman who thought Pete was a hustler and paid him twenty dollars. He met a kid who had been in jail for selling drugs and lived in a rich old man's attic but they had to lock the door to keep him from coming in and he kept scratching at the door and mumbling strange things. None of these people ever made plans to see Pete again. And he had to be completely secret about the football player he met on the fourth floor whose note said he liked to pose and Pete's note back said he was an artist. They never had sex but Pete had gone to his room several times, and once one of his teammates was there and they demonstrated wrestling holds in their jock-straps and chose their favorite drawings but let Pete keep the rest. It was frustrating but worth it.

But Pete had also begun to feel he would never find someone to fall in love with. He always had plenty of good advice for Russ but none for himself, and to Susie he had to pretend he had actually never thought of these things before. He had stopped expecting his desires to change. Now they were stronger. He had worried Mom and Dad by saying he might not even pass his January exams. Of course he would do fine, but he somehow no longer cared as much and wanted his parents to realize that.

Then when his last semester began he made a sudden decision to apply to art school. Mac and Don were relieved. They had stopped trying to figure out their roommate, but they always kept his drawings in case he became famous as they claimed to believe he would. They called them "our Persian portraits." Pete knew those drawings were more intimate than the snapshots of their various girlfriends they taped up over their desks. They proved how Pete's eyes had once studied their faces and chests and rumps and thighs, the frizzy mop, the lengthening ponytail. He called them exercises in light and shadow, but they were really his way of remembering. He still drew them once in a while. There was one of Mac asleep on the oriental rug by their hearth, his cheek smudged into his forearm, which was glowing in the firelight.

Gay Party

One of the English tutors, who occasionally sat down by Pete at lunch, asked him to join some other students for coffee in his room. They all sat about on his leather couch and leather chairs carefully holding their cups and saucers. Hanging on the wall was a beautiful but lifeless plaster face whose closed eyelids seemed to stare at Pete while he sipped his creamy and sugary Boston-style coffee. Pete hardly knew the other students. They were into poetry and drama and all seemed to share a witty joke no one had actually told but only referred to in sly asides and double entendres.

Pete asked Dr. Abrams whose face that was on the wall. One sophomore rolled his eyes, and a boy with a languid voice said, "It's Keats's death mask. Jordan has it at precisely the poet's height. Keats was even shorter than you are, Peter." Then Dr. Abrams said, "Peter is quite tall enough," but the admonishment did not settle the others down nor make Pete feel any surer of himself. These were the people he had naturally avoided for over three years.

Another time Dr. Abrams stayed at the table with Pete when their fellow diners had left and Pete was still on his lemon pie. They talked about the Museum of Fine Arts and the Gardner, and then Dr. Abrams said, "But you should see more of Boston than its art." He suggested Pete come with him to a party two of his friends were giving. Without anything more being said Pete began to imagine what kind of party it might be.

It was in a brick townhouse on the flat side of Charles Street that was like the Ulysses S. Grant house in Galena where Gramma and Lemuel had once taken him and John on a rainy boring Saturday many summers ago. Each room was filled with dark Victorian furniture, heavy closed curtains, flowery wallpaper, leather-bound books within glass doors, and rugs laid over rugs. Everyone at the party was male. Some wore sport coats and ties, some mod shirts and bellbottoms. Pete wore his usual plaid flannel shirt and wheat jeans.

He was surprised when Dr. Abrams did not stick beside him. After handing Pete a whiskey sour he went off to talk to some other Harvard types. This is my first gay party, Pete thought. It was nothing like the party Mac and Don had taken him and John to where people slobbed around smoking and playing music and barely talking except for one loudmouth philosophizing in a corner. John had thought it was cool, but Pete found it surprisingly dumb.

Now here he was standing next to a sweet-looking boy in tennis shoes, tight jeans, and an olive green Army surplus jacket. Motown was playing on the second floor, and the boy asked Pete if he wanted to go up. He was Charlie, he said. Pete downed his drink and climbed the narrow stairs. He was nervous, but after a few songs he realized he was no worse a dancer than Charlie, and then they ended up sitting on an uncomfortable velvet loveseat in an alcove and, because they had seen other couples kissing as they danced, wrapped their arms around each other and spent the next hour making out.

A Real Boyfriend

The others were in the waves, but Pete had stayed on his towel to heat up first. It was late June and getting warmer each day. One of their crowd had brought the morning paper. It flapped in the breeze when Pete opened it, but before he could fold it up again he read that actress Jayne Mansfield had been killed in a car crash. The details were gruesome. He tucked the paper under the beer cooler and remembered his own water bottle Jayne. The paint at the tips of her breasts had worn off, and he had used his acrylics to re-blacken the pink spots. Pete had never actually filled her with hot water. She had stood on his shelf between the Yale football helmet and his car collection.

It was ten years since he and Russ had seen the real Jayne in *Will Success Spoil Rock Hunter?* When Dad picked them up he had ribbed them about it and must have told Aunt Helena that Pete had a thing for Jayne Mansfield. Now that Dad knew about him and Charlie he had told Aunt Helena too and she had sent Pete a muscleboy card from Greenwich Village that said, "Dahling, I love you so-o-o-o much!" Charlie could not believe Pete had such an understanding family.

They were spending a week on the Cape at Kenneth and Brian's house. They met other boys on the beach and in the bars and the ones Brian had over. Down here everyone was always looking at each other. They kept discussing who was cute and guessing who did what with whom. Pete had never had such conversations or been able to touch a boy and be touched back in front of other people the way he and Charlie did. They even once had sex in the same room as another couple with the lights just low enough to see what was going on in the other bed.

You were expected to act flirty no matter what a person looked like, and though it sounded silly Pete was almost getting used to the word *gay*. Mostly he simply liked having people think of him and Charlie as being together. When he had finally told Mac and Don about it they said they were not entirely surprised, it was so extremely cool and Persian of Pete. When his parents visited for graduation Charlie even came out to dinner with them in his pink sweater instead of his Army surplus. Mom had been nervous but nice, and Dad had acted as if Charlie was just another Mac or Don. When they walked back to the hotel Dad had whispered, "But go easy on the specifics, buddy, because she's your mom and she's a woman." And next morning at breakfast

Mom had told Pete not to let Dad's worries worry him, that she was perfectly fine and only worried whether John should know yet, but she had liked Charlie and why not bring him home for a visit at the end of summer.

Now Charlie was out there in the waves splashing the pale boy they had met last night named Arnie. Pete felt a thump in his heart. Brian had said Arnie would let anyone do anything to him. This morning Charlie had kidded around that he and Pete were going to make themselves an Arnie sandwich for lunch. This beach was huge, this ocean was huge, men's bodies were everywhere Pete looked. Yesterday down at the far end a nude man had got an erection when they stopped to look at his sandcastle. He said they all three should go back into the dunes, but instead Charlie and Pete had kept walking along the shore holding hands.

And here came Arnie running out of the water dripping and squealing, "Get ya boyfriend offa me!" He plunged into the sand next to Pete. Pete grabbed him by the tiny red suit that was slipping off his skinny ass and held his wrists till Charlie got there. Soon they were in a squirming pile up kicking at the sand and tickling each other. Charlie must have felt Pete was tickling Arnie too much because suddenly he pressed a hard kiss onto Pete's lips. Arnie fell off to one side pretending to welcome his freedom.

On the Breakwater

It was not because of Arnie. It had started to feel as if it were everything. It was even because Pete would not call Arnie "she" the way the others did. The more embarrassed Pete got the more stubborn he felt. Brian said, "What's with her?" and then, "Loosen up, Mary." Charlie just laughed. Pete tried to joke about being an uptight Midwestern Harvard grad but made the mistake of adding that he did not see why if you liked men you would refer to yourselves as women. So they took to calling him "the man" or "our man" or "Manly Man" or simply "Man." They thought it was hysterical. "Just because he's hung," said Arnie, "he thinks he isn't one of the girls."

Then Kenneth, who had given the party where Pete and Charlie met, came down at the end of the week. He and Brian began acting pissy about all these kids drifting through their house, tracking sand in and raiding the ice-box. "Okay, babies, time to clean up your act," said Brian. "Colonel Ken has arrived."

Charlie started washing the dishes, and Arnie waltzed around doing his houseboy routine, dusting and polishing to no particular effect. Pete was unsure what he should do or say. Kenneth had sat down next to him on the couch. Pete was staring at his own bare knees. In his new stretchy bathing suit he felt especially naked next to long-limbed Kenneth, still in white shirt and slacks from work.

"But, Bri," Kenneth said and touched Pete's bare shoulder, "maybe this one's worth all the mess."

"He's spoken for, sweetie pie," said Brian. "Miss Palmolive over there has him wrapped around her—or maybe Miss Olive's lips are wrapped around his—oh well, who knows? Or cares?"

Kenneth made a tired face. Then he said to Pete in a comradely tone, "I work all week and this is supposed to be my entertainment?"

"Excuse me, Manly Man," said Arnie tickling Pete's knees with his feather duster. "And what may I get you, sir?" he asked Kenneth.

"A nice stiff—"

"Martini!" squealed Brian, who was dancing about with the cocktail shaker.

"Oh, is that what you call it?" said Arnie, eyelids lowered, lips in a pout. "That means on the beach I almost had two martinis at once!"

"Tee martoonies," Brian announced. Pete could tell he was trying to loosen up his grumpy lover, but

Kenneth just took the glass. Brian sat on the other side of Pete with a second glass. He did not offer one to Pete.

Then one of the other boys, Richard, came back from the beach with a guy nobody knew, and Pete could hear him at the front door saying, "I share this place with some other queens," and then, "Oh!" when he saw Kenneth and Brian glaring at him.

Brian held his martini glass below his lips and said, like a schoolmarm, "Kenneth and Brian have kindly allowed me to stay at their well-appointed beach house and bring tricks back for quick meaningless sex."

The trick, a dark young man with a tidy mustache, was checking everyone out while Richard's face turned red.

"Repeat after me," Brian prompted. "Kenneth and Brian—"

"Kenneth and Brian," said Richard.

"Have kindly allowed me—"

So it went for the evening. Drinking made Kenneth quieter and somewhat fierce-looking and Brian got campier. Eventually Richard went upstairs with his trick but half an hour later did not manage to sneak him out. "And where do you two gentlemen think you're going?" asked Brian.

Pete did not want to hear the answer. Charlie was still mad at him for not helping do dishes but was nevertheless willing to go up and make out on the roof deck. Pete began to feel better. Then Kenneth and Brian and Richard and the trick all came up with margaritas and started getting naked in the starlight. On the second floor someone else was fucking Arnie. They could all hear the rhythmic "hoonh! hoonh! hoonh!" Pete was still holding onto Charlie, but he could see the trick licking Charlie's ankle and then working his way up to tongue at his crotch. Charlie began passionately kissing Pete's mouth, but despite his own hard-on Pete said he was really tired and somehow got disentangled so he could ease himself down the steep stairs. He heard Brian calling, "Hey, Manly, bring your big shlong back up here!"

Early the next morning Pete slipped out by himself and walked toward the end of town and out onto the long breakwater. He sat for hours looking across the flat still bay feeling cramped up inside. By eleven Charlie came looking for him and told him in his Boston accent to stop being such a "spoilspawt." That last syllable sounded suddenly foreign to Pete.

"It was too weird for me," Pete said.

"What, the aw-gee?"

"I'm not good at orgies," Pete said.

"What, not inta olda men? Ya'll be old too some day, ya know, Pete Hahvahd Fuckin' Dabney. Besides, that guy with the mustache was only twenty-six. He did everybody one afta the otha."

"I didn't feel like it."

"He really wanted to do you, Pete. He said so. So who was screwin' Ahnie anyways?"

"I don't know. He left." Pete kept looking across the bay at the horizon where the city would be.

"So maybe it's a new thing, Pete," Charlie said. "Look, bein' hawny doesn't mean we can't love each otha the most."

Pete would not respond.

Charlie gave him a long stare. "So what did they actually teach ya at cawlege?"

Pete did not actually know what he knew. He had not had enough chance to learn it. He had never seriously discussed or even read about any of this. "I can't talk anymore, Charlie," he finally said. He was afraid he would cry.

Later on it all turned into a kind of panic. Without telling anyone he took the ferry back to Boston.

Home

"Want to talk about it, buddy?" Dad asked when Mom had taken John for a repeat of his driver's test.

"I'm sorry to have put you and Mom through it," Pete said.

From the back porch they heard the neighborhood sounds Pete had almost forgotten: a clicking and whirring lawn mower being pushed one way then the other, the snap of clippers, a splattering hose with little kids screaming, a pounding hammer. The sticky air made Pete not want to move or think. Before he and Dad sat down they had poured themselves lemonades. Pete could tell Dad wanted him to talk more, but he could not come up with anything new. They had never had conversations like this. Pete took a long sip from his glass.

"Let me put it this way," Dad said. "You didn't get to practice the way your buddies did, so now it comes out a little rougher."

Pete thought of all the sexual things he had been doing for so many years that he would never tell his dad about, but still maybe it was true about having no practice.

"This is what a broken heart feels like, Pete," Dad said. "John's had a couple though never quite as bad. He'll be a good brother to you. Mom just wants to wait to explain till he gets his license, but he knows you're feeling low."

Pete was listening thankfully. He wished Dad would keep talking. He was taking it more seriously than Pete did, as if there had been a real love affair instead of a pathetic mistake. Pete had so stupidly imagined it was serious and real, and he had made Dad and Mom think so too. He had called them at the worst moment. He had come back from the Cape to the room he was subletting in a house of old people he did not know. He had sat there alone for days not really expecting Charlie to show up again. His parents suggested he call Don since he was still in Boston. Pete went over for a family meal before Don went into the Coast Guard. Mac was back in Philadelphia, so Pete wrote him. Mac and Don were used to breakups. If only he had not made such a thing of it to his parents.

Restraint

"Good evening," said Kenneth. "Come in. You look refreshed. I'm glad you called." Pete stepped into the vestibule then followed Kenneth upstairs to the living room where the dancing had been. "No one's here. Brian's still on the Cape. I haven't seen your little friend. Would you like lemonade? A beer? It's so hot, maybe a cold beer.

Pete's first words were "thank you."

Kenneth was very tall, hawk-eyed and hawk-nosed. Charlie had said he "came from money." When Kenneth first picked up Charlie on the Esplanade they had apparently played some interesting kinky games. Hearing about it had upset Pete back when he was in love, but now he was curious.

Kenneth said nothing more about the time on the Cape. He did ask briefly about Pete's trip to Chicago and his art school plans and the studio apartment he had found for the fall. Then as if it was part of the same conversation Kenneth said he was intrigued by the visual effect his tall body would have next to Pete's short one. "As an artist you understand the appeal of contrasts," he said. "I'm six eight, and you must be—"

"Five six," said Pete.

"Don't you find it a turn on?"

"You're very tall," Pete said.

"My idea about being queer," Kenneth said, "is that it goes best when the hetero thing is in a way replicated —tall and short, young and old, black and white, rich and poor. Most queers tend to go out looking for themselves, but how boring!"

"You're probably right," Pete said. He put down his beer and let his arms hang over the back of the chair he was sitting in, tightening his T-shirt against his chest instead of hunching forward the way he usually did. It was strange for Pete to be the one looked at instead of the one who did the looking.

Kenneth was watching him with his hawk eyes. Pete stretched back a little more the way he imagined Charlie must have. Kenneth said, "You know I could tie your arms behind you like that, yes, the very way you're sitting."

"Oh," said Pete bringing his arms back around into his lap.

"Have you never been restrained? It's not what you might fear. It's a matter of being kept from fully responding, from being allowed to touch back. It makes every inch of skin tingle. It drives your whole body crazy. I'll use only the softest bonds, a silk bathrobe tie, velvet curtain tiebacks, nothing you can't get out of."

Pete followed Kenneth up to the third floor bedrooms. He felt he was returning to a world where all was dimly lit and safe.

Life Class

In their first class the drawing instructor, a pear-shaped bald man with arching eyebrows, had said to them, "Art is long, life is short, so what are you going to do about it?" The class had not known if they were supposed to answer, but after a tense pause he continued: "There's your short lives to consider. Better not waste what little you've got. And then, friends, there's art. Art is meant to look better and better as time passes. The artist has seen something no one has seen quite that way before. The hoi polloi take their sweet time before realizing how sharp the artist's eye has been. You say, well, you understand Picasso, but then you've all grown up with him. How many of you will manage to see what Picasso himself in his old age still hasn't seen? Nobody in this room, myself included, most likely. But I have asked the question. So that's the end of my lecture.

Now you'll all do some drawing, and we'll see where we're starting from. Today's subject?"

A plain looking woman at the side of the room stood up, and Pete saw she was wearing only a bathrobe. She dropped it to the floor and sat on a high stool at the front of the class. Pete had never before seen a woman entirely naked. He was glad the first model was not a man. It would be easier to see exactly what he saw and not what he wished for.

After class he and his classmate Cynthia walked down the avenue for pizza. Pete had not minded the instructor's attitude the way Cynthia had. "You probably got lots of blowhards at Harvard," she said. "I don't have the patience for it."

"I never had much to say in college," Pete admitted. "I had to study hard, but I got by."

"I fucked around and did fabulously," said Cynthia with a toss of her straight blondish hair. By "fucked around" she really meant "fucked off" because at their first supper she had told Pete she never had dates in college. She was a pale, dumpling-faced girl who wore long jeans skirts and peasant blouses and kept her fingernails stubby.

"What gives you your confidence, Cynthia?" He sensed she needed his compliments.

"His clever act didn't get past me," she said, a slice of pepperoni and mushroom at her lips. "It's technique I want. I'll deal with the meaning of art by myself."

"The strange thing is I always had smart friends," Pete said.

"Your roommates sounded like typical entitled dumb Harvard jerk assholes."

"I should've gone to art school right off," Pete said sadly.

"Either way you'd've been getting experiences," Cynthia said with a firm shake of her head. "I don't regret college. This regret thing has to go."

"You don't regret?"

"I complain, but I don't regret."

Pete took a second slice. To him Cynthia seemed full of regret. It caused him to want to make sure she did not get hurt. He had felt the same about that afternoon's model sitting calm and naked on that stool. He wondered if his sketches had expressed a wish not to expose her. He had found an angle where her arm obscured her breasts and her raised thigh shielded her pubic hair. Was he the one made shy by what he saw not she by what she was showing? But Pete was in art school now. He was there to learn to see things.

The Flat Drawn World

Pete was thinking of his earliest drawings and of what drawing had meant to him when he was small. Whenever he saw a thing he liked or maybe did not like but felt something about he had found his hand wanting to move across paper. It was all in the moving of his hand—as if it did the thinking so his eyes could watch.

He remembered his drawing of Bill Rice, the boy in his swimming class. Pete's hand moving across the paper was a way of touching Bill Rice when he could not otherwise have imagined touching him. Since then Pete had touched many boys and men but some still not, not Mac or Don, though he had drawn them often, not Talcott except once. He had never drawn the two of them on that ridge after Talcott kissed him. His only later drawing of Talcott was a senior caricature for the yearbook, and then Pete had hidden him behind an oversized tenor saxophone. Those caricatures were meant as affectionate insults. Susie had drawn one of Pete bent over his sketchbook with wide Sal Mineo eyes staring up at you. That was how Pete looked to people, his hand moving on its own while his eyes glanced up at his subject and then down at his art. It showed how Pete lived in two worlds.

Now at art school he lived mostly in the flat drawn world and found it comforting. He was with others who also lived in that world instead of being the only one there. He did not always like or understand what his classmates drew, even what Cynthia drew though he praised her, and they never said much about Pete's work at all. He drew men in ways that unsettled them, all except Cynthia, but his eyes and his right hand and his left as it rubbed and erased and tilted the paper were telling him what to put there. Once he saw, not in life but in memories of pick-ups in the Fens, a big man sprawled on a shabby couch with one thick leg bent at the knee, a muscled arm flung over the head, stretching, a man sleeping after sex, satisfied and exhausted. Pete's classmates passed over it because of what they did not want to know about Pete.

The Pale Horizon

Pete had not seen the ocean since taking the ferry back
from the Cape. He forgot the ocean was near. But at
home for Christmas he went down to Lake Michigan
and painted canvasboards of the gray, blue, white, flat
horizon with nothing beyond it. He felt cold sitting in
the sand. He worked quickly, fingers twiddling in his
mittens to keep warm, fast brushstrokes, smears of the
palette knife, a half dozen small canvasboards he could
surround himself with back in his old bedroom.

He and his family had crossed the lake on the
Wisconsin car ferry when he was young. Halfway to
Michigan they could see neither shore. Somehow in the
middle of the country they were out of sight of land. On
the top deck small Pete had slowly turned, eyes on the
pale horizon, from east all the way around to west and
back. He imagined all the dry earth had floated off in

every direction leaving only one boat and these seagulls. It was their last family trip to Grandfather's cottage in Indian River before he sold it. John could not have been more than a baby.

Pete wondered if these paintings of the empty winter lake or his landscapes of Gramma's summer meadow, even the views out windows he had lived behind, if they belonged at all with his portraits, his nudes, which had no more background than a rug or a chair or a bed. His landscapes had no people in them except maybe tiny distant shapes. Pete had drawn Talcott on the tractor with himself riding the hitch but for background he only put a ray of setting sunlight and a line of treetops. Even his car portraits had little more than the frame of a garage door or the rut of a road. Pete decided when he returned for his next semester he would find a way to let his people and his cars sit in a world around them. He did fear they might lose outline, but Pete had been closely studying Cézanne who showed him there was a way bodies were part of the earth and also that the earth or fruit or a glass bottle were like bodies. Pete had not quite seen that before, but now it was obvious. No wonder his classmates found his work too simple. It took him so long to see things as a whole.

It had got very cold and windy, so Pete slipped his canvasboards into the slots in the carrying box Mom and Dad had given him for Christmas and headed to Mom's Dart he had left parked on the pier.

Family Politics

Grandmother had always preferred John. It did not matter that in two years he was heading to Madison not New Haven. After Grandfather died Grandmother forgot about those things. She needed Doreen's help to keep her mind on one thing at a time. It was easy to think about John because he still lived at home while her other grandsons, Pete and Maurice, lived far away. John knew how Gramma had always preferred Pete, so he kept Grandmother for himself even after she got so vague.

But John was glad when Pete came along because then he could be the one to explain to Pete what Grandmother meant and to show Pete where things were kept in her kitchen. Pete enjoyed watching his brother being different from the way he was with Mom and Dad or his friends.

"Grandmother needs her slipper socks," John told Doreen. The wind off the lake was blowing at the rattling windows. Some years ago Grandfather had stopped remodeling or doing repairs, and by now the whole house seemed old fashioned and off kilter. Pete felt the wind creeping in. "And here's your shawl," John said as he draped it around Grandmother's shoulders.

"Helena lives in New York City among homosexuals," Grandmother said.

John looked quickly at Pete's smile then said, "Not exactly, Grandmother. She has her own apartment. There's all sort of types in New York."

"Pete does not live in New York," Grandmother said.

"No, I live in Cambridge."

"Pete lives in Cambridge, Massachusetts, and Maurice and Aunt Helena live in New York City, and I live here with Mom and Dad less than a mile away."

"Paul and Rachel live in New York City."

"No, they live here. I live with them. I'm still in high school."

"It's much colder here," Grandmother said.

"Here's your slippers," John said taking them from Doreen who then went off to the beauty parlor while the grandsons took over. She was getting old too.

Pete watched his long-haired little brother bending down to remove the pink bedroom slippers and pull up the slipper socks over their grandmother's small pale feet. The moccasin soles and the bright red and black Indian pattern in the knitting looked odd hanging out of her pink bathrobe. Grandmother put her hand in John's hair and lifted his floppy bangs and let them fall back to his forehead. She did not mind that he was a flower child. His orange and blue mod shirt did not bother her. Pete's gray wool sweater and raggedy corduroys probably looked stranger to her now.

"I'm going to make tea," John said. When John and his friends spoke of "tea" they meant something else by it, and it amazed Pete how John could put all that aside when they were at Grandmother's. "Pete's going to stay and talk to you," John said.

Bare tree branches were waving in the wind outside the window behind Grandmother's head. "You voted for Lyndon Johnson," she said.

"I couldn't vote then, but I did wear the buttons."

"I voted for Barry Goldwater."

"I'm sure you did," said Pete.

"He's Jewish," Grandmother said.

"And you voted for him anyway," Pete said.

"Lyndon Johnson is giving it all to the Negroes."

"Well, not all," said Pete.

"And the Red Chinese," she added. "I don't like to see his big ears and his droopy nose on my television." Then she changed her tone and said in a sweet voice, "Could you turn it back on, dear?"

John did not let her watch television during his visits, but Pete did not know what else to do so he turned it on for now, and in silence they watched a cowboy movie until John brought in the tea tray with the pound cake he had brought. He set it down, but before he poured from the pot he snapped off the TV and said, "Grandmother, you'll have plenty of time for that later."

"He's strict with me," she told Pete.

The Starving Artist

When Maurice came to Boston for his bank Pete sat in his hotel lobby dreading their meeting. It was an hour of self-conscious waiting before his cousin appeared in a business suit, apologized for being late, looked at Pete's jeans, and said, "I see you haven't grown up yet. Well, I suppose you're an artist. Mother lets them get away with everything." Maurice was twenty-six now and divorced after a short marriage. He was being transferred to Houston.

They went to the hotel bar for dinner on Maurice's expense account. "Because you're the starving artist," he said and passed the peanut bowl. "I can't imagine what you subsist on. I suggest you find an effete old gentleman for a patron. He won't expect all that much in return. But when your Gramma Tice dies I suppose you'll be set up anyway. Unfortunately I only got one set of grandparents. Never saw my Lavallee ones. Strange having a name I've had nothing ever to do with. In Houston they'll think I'm a Cajun."

Pete mentioned his own unlikely birthplace of Leesville, Louisiana. His parents were at Camp Polk before Dad went overseas.

"My dad had skedaddled by then," said Maurice. "Strange you being a quasi-Southerner because of the war."

"And then I came home and lived with only Mom until I was one and a half. Gramma lived with us in the winter, and we lived out with her in the summer until Dad got back."

Glasses of Scotch were set before them, the Glenfiddich Maurice had requested. He sipped appreciatively, and Pete tried to like it. Maurice was beginning to seem less unpleasant.

"Do you remember anything about the war?" Pete asked.

"We're in a war right now, cousin. You haven't noticed?"

"But what do you remember?"

"How would I remember? I wasn't even five when it ended. But actually I do remember being with Grandfather and Grandmother the day Roosevelt died. They were celebrating, and my mother of course was screaming at them. My very first memory. Way to start off a childhood. I remember not one thing of Raymond Lavallee."

"Just as well?" Pete asked, and Maurice nodded and sipped. He cast his eyes over the menu and suggested raw oysters first then something red and juicy to put some meat on Pete's bones.

Decadence

Pete got a long rambling letter from Mac in Philadelphia where he was working in the projects and going to social work school at night. Mac admitted he missed Don and Pete too. Don had had his frizz shaved off in the Coast Guard, ha-ha! Mac's handwriting slanted different directions and got bigger and smaller as though he was writing on a jiggly bus. He said he was worried about the draft. He thought Don was crazy to think the Coast Guard was the easy way to get it over with. The Coast Guard was still part of the fucking system. He said Pete would probably get some student deferment or maybe go 4F, but he should think seriously about these things. Mac worried that Pete's Persian proclivities, as he called them, might numb him to what was really happening out there. Pete might get too decadent and not face up to things. Decadence, Mac said, is great for a period of your youth, but most people can't afford that luxury. Pete should see how drugs and prostitution are undermining the lives of black people. And venereal disease, babe, he said. It felt less like a kindly warning than a rebuke. Pete had to put the letter down for a minute before he could read on.

He was sitting at the card table he used for meals and desk work. It fit into his kitchenette under the window with room for two folding chairs. Last night Pete had sat there in his bathrobe having tea with a Portuguese boy he had met along the river. Even after sex the boy had his bare feet up under the robe making Pete hard again. In his earlier life Pete would have fallen completely in love.

Mac's letter now had an orange juice stain from the sticky tabletop shining right through the page. "I might go to Canada," Mac wrote. "This is a crossroads. I grew up with everything but there are people living a few miles from my parents who have practically nothing. People in Laos and Vietnam have even less. I'm more of a Communist every day, Pete, I'm not afraid to say so. I wish you could devote your art to the people, Pete. I know you have to study and learn but just please don't go decadent, promise me. Sleep with whomever you love but don't avoid the real work out there. Art can help a revolution, Pete. Art can help people think new thoughts and not be only pretty scenes and pretty bodies but show real suffering in real people."

Pete knew Mac was right, but he did not know what to write him back. Mac would not understand the suffering in Pete's paintings. He would see them as decadent, Pete's naked men and his landscapes, despite how they struggled for solid form on their flat planes trying to become part of the world.

Older and Tougher

The Portuguese boy Manny came back a number of times wanting Pete to fuck him and fuck him and fuck him. Pete was used to it the other way around, but it was exciting to act like someone older and tougher. The same thing had happened once back in senior year with a soft pink and white Northeastern student who took Pete to his rented room. There was a clawfoot tub in the bathroom down his hall. In hot soapy water the boy sat down onto Pete's cock and kissed him wildly the whole time they were fucking. The boy had two tickets to Bob Dylan that night. Later Pete had to pretend he had gone with a Radcliffe friend so he could tell Mac and Don how all the folk fans booed when Dylan came out with an electric guitar and a rock band. Don approved of "Like a Rolling Stone," but Mac was getting into twelve-string Delta blues and no longer bothered with the folk rock controversy.

Pete and his roommates had heard a lot of music together. Junior year they had driven to Worcester in Don's dad's car to see the Rolling Stones, and they had seen the Animals at the high school auditorium in Cambridge, but what Pete really loved was the Supremes up close at Blinstrub's night club. He loved the supple, sensual Motown tunes more than hard-driving edgy white music. Now in his little apartment with his easel at the double window looking into the trees across Chestnut Street he seldom played the radio. Manny made him listen to the Portuguese show, and Pete liked the songs but wondered what they were about. Manny himself was really more of a Peggy Lee fan.

Manny worked in linens at Jordan Marsh. He was obsessed with ruffled curtains and huge fluffy towels and bedspreads with flowery patterns and brightly striped sheets. He could get Pete discounts. Pete explained that as an artist he needed to live in plain surroundings so he could focus on his painting. Manny said he liked it that Pete was no femme. He loved telling Pete about his room at home and how he had done up his mother's and sisters' rooms too. "I wish you would fuck me all night in my fabulous bed," he said. "It would be my biggest thrill." But he worked long hours and his mother was always home, so Pete never got to do what Manny dreamed of.

When warm weather came Pete met a rough-looking man on the riverbank who invited him to his apartment up past Harvard Square. There would be a note on the door and Pete should follow instructions. Pete waited the half hour and then walked over. The note said, "Hi

Jimmy—I've had to go out—you must be beat after your long trip so have a long nap—the plumber may come to fix the drip in the kitchen—see you tonight—Uncle Jack." The sofa bed was pulled out, so Pete took off his clothes and lay down under the white sheet. Soon the door opened and the same man came in wearing a tool belt. He went straight to the kitchen and started banging around. After ten minutes Jimmy decided to yawn, and the plumber called out, "Sorry to wake you, kid." He leaned in the doorway and talked about the heat then sat on the edge of the bed and stared at a particular lump in the sheet. He let his hand brush against it.

After being given poppers and getting intensely fucked Jimmy had no idea if he was now to become Pete again. And who was his Uncle Jack? Uncle Jack seemed to read books in Italian and German and play J. S. Bach on his harpsichord.

Juried Show

Pete and Cynthia were in their first juried show. Pete had two pieces, Cynthia three. Hers formed a series of increasingly mud-like collages embedded with women's screaming faces. All she gave away were the titles— "1965," "1966," and "1967"—but she was happy to discuss her technique with anyone who asked.

Pete did not talk well about technique. The things he saw made him use paint in different ways, but he could not explain why. He only knew when it looked right emerging on the canvas. Like Cynthia he limited himself to titles. His two paintings in the show were "From Delacroy to David" and "Goodbye, Charlie."

"Delacroy?" inquired a tall beaky woman holding a plastic cup of white wine and a cracker smeared with Camembert cheese.

"I'm Delacroy, I guess," Pete said. "That's David."

"But you're Peter Dabney," said the woman looking at the card below the painting. "How do you do? I'm Jane—" Her last name got lost in the chatter around them. She gestured helplessly with her full hands, so Pete's hands went behind his back again. He felt shorter than usual beside this tall woman. "You're homosexual?" she asked. "It's good to see a man painting men. Or have I presumed too much?"

Pete shook his head but must have been blushing.

"Your paintings don't avoid anything," Jane said, her eyes hovering close to each canvas, studying Charlie's buttocks, running down David's arm past his nipples to the curve of his hip. "But they don't overdo it," she said. "Neither an indeterminate squiggle nor a bold upstanding prick."

Pete thought he had heard her right but was not sure enough to say anything, so he gave a noncommittal smile.

"A man in repose is not the same as a woman in repose," Jane said close into Pete's ear. "An unaroused man usually needs a fig leaf or loincloth or codpiece not to seem vulnerable and ineffectual." She was amusing herself, so Pete tried an equivalent laugh. "What's remarkable about David here," she said pointing so as to draw into their conversation another young man in a flowered shirt who had been passing along the wall and pausing at each piece, "is that"—Jane shot a knowing glance at the young man and said, "Now that's a penis! It's luxuriating. Only a homosexual would paint it that way. Oh, I'm sorry—"

The young man in the flowered shirt with long reddish hair had been listening earnestly. Now Jane had been called away by a fat bearded man with a plastic cup of red wine in each hand, so he turned to look more closely at the painting of David and then at Pete.

Cézanne

As an undergraduate Pete had loved Ingres. In art school he found that Ingres was particularly "out" except in the estimation of his drawing teacher, who promised him Ingres would soon enough be coming back "in." Pete found his own work passing into a new phase. Its classical foundation—the Ingres influence—was harder to discern, but he knew it was still there helping him see and shape and balance what lay under his messier, brighter, less thought-out surfaces. Pete had become entranced with Cézanne. In college he had not yet understood him from within, which was the way Cézanne had to be understood. Pete now studied the series of the *Boy in a Red Waistcoat*, especially the watercolor with the collar undone and the big hands in the lap, the arrangement more than the beauty of the figure. He wanted to paint Ben like that. In exchange for posing Ben asked Pete to pose for him as well.

They had gone for coffee after the opening reception, and it came out that Ben was an artist too, a photographer. He had not let on at the show because he was new at it. He said he did not have Pete's gift, could not draw at all, but he thought he had a sense for the right moment to catch things on film. He was studying the book on the Zone System, which gave his black-and-white prints a range of sun and shadow Pete had never seen before in photographs. The rough surfaces of rocks in a streambed were like a field of stars in a black night. A small boy danced on an expanse of gravel, kicking, bending, and casting unexpected patterns of blur and shade. A wind billowed a pair of sunlit linen curtains into a darkened room, the blacks so black, the whites so white.

Though Pete was painting Ben clothed, as Cézanne did the *Boy in a Red Waistcoat*, Ben wanted to photograph Pete nude but curled up tightly with his head between his knees. It was odd to be naked for someone but not for sex. It was too matter of fact to give Pete an erection. In one shot the smooth surface of his seemingly neckless back looked like a bell pepper, pointy shoulders up top, small round buttocks to rest on. Pete had never modeled before and asked Ben never to say whose body it was, especially not to Jane when he showed her his portfolio. She had promised to connect Ben to a few other galleries because she did not hang photographs in hers. She had already sold Charlie and David and was eager now for the portrait of Ben.

There were no summer courses at school, only free studio. You were expected to do a ton of unsupervised work to get ready for the second year. People stayed up all night. However late Pete set off for home there was always someone still working. He did not know what to do about the Fens now, these gatherings in the reeds, pairs, threesomes, whole circles of men. He was tempted, especially because Ben still wanted to wait till they really knew each other. Walking through late at night Pete did partake sometimes but not with the excitement of last spring. All around him men were reaching for each other, kneeling down, or bending over. No one said anything at all and it was too dark to see who anyone was, but Pete kept seeing Ben. Ben would not think this was fun. Ben, with his thick long reddish hair and pale skin, had stared with blue eyes straight at Pete and told him he was falling in love with him.

Going Through Everything

That July Pete flew home for Grandmother's funeral, and everyone wanted him to stay, especially Aunt Helena who was going through everything in the old house. Maurice had to get back to Houston, so she was alone now. But Pete also needed to get back to his work and, though he did not tell anyone, to Ben. It meant he would miss August out at Gramma's for the first time in his life.

Mom had been acting strange the whole time he was home. It was the end of her having to deal with Dad's parents, and it meant she and Dad would now have a lot more money, but she could not mention that so she told sweet stories about Grandmother to Pete and John. Then John told some stories of the crazy stuff Grandmother had said toward the end, which got Mom going on the outrageous things Grandmother use to say about Negroes and Jews and Democrats, and they all finally could laugh, as if with the old lady gone that was the end of those sorts of attitudes. Dad did not mind as long as they kept it humorous, but Pete could see in his downcast eyes that he was already missing his mother more than he had ever missed his father.

John missed Grandmother too. After the funeral he had woven himself a necklace of flowers from her garden and said he would not take it off even when it withered. He would let its petals fall and its stems untwine in their own good time. He, not Pete, would be helping Aunt Helena organize things. He was just at the age Aunt Helena appreciated, going into his last year of high school and on the verge of everything. Pete was too old. His aunt loved him and hugged him and cried and said he had to come stay with her soon in New York and walk through their museums and discover new galleries, but Pete could see her eyes brighten more whenever John talked about his latest girlfriend Laurie.

One late afternoon Mom was having her gin and tonic alone on the back porch because Dad was still with Aunt Helena and the lawyers. John had gone off on a long serious walk with Laurie. Pete came out with a gin and tonic of his own and asked Mom how she was doing.

"Mostly I worry about you," she said.

It was not what Pete had expected. He assured her he was fine, loved art school, loved doing his work, was as happy as he had ever been.

"But if you would like to see a psychologist, Pete, or a psychiatrist, analyst, I mean, whatever might help get some perspective—I don't mean as something to change you but to help you work all this out better. Dad and I would really like to pay for it, it would make us feel so much more relaxed about you, we feel there's so little we can do."

Their Rules

Ben was standing at the gate as Pete walked across the hot tarmac toward his grinning face. He knew they could not kiss until they were alone again. They went to the men's room, but it was too crowded, so they stood at adjacent urinals without even glancing down then washed their hands and quickly caught each other's eye in the mirror.

At least there was plenty to talk about like regular friends on the subway to Central Square. Ben had made sandwiches for a late lunch. He lived above a furniture store on Mass. Ave. in an apartment with filthy gray carpeting and huge smoked-up windows and a high ceiling peeling off long curls of gray paint. An old fridge and a two-burner gas stove stood on a square of yellowing linoleum, and the sink was around the corner in the windowless bathroom he also used as a darkroom. The main room had only his lumpy mattress on the floor, his tripods and lights and a roll of backdrop paper hung on one wall, and a long work table littered with photography books and dirty clothes. There was a cleared space for the two of them to sit on little stools.

But first they fell on the mattress and got to their hugs and kisses and felt their whole bodies close and sweaty in summer's mugginess. They kicked their sandals off, then unbuttoned their shirts, and Pete again felt the greater urge he was trying not to satisfy. He licked Ben's flat white chest and gently sucked his pinkish nipples. When they rolled over Ben sucked hard on Pete's browner ones till they tingled. He slurped at the hair in Pete's armpits. He stuck his tongue into Pete's ear and made him squirm. Pete struggled to get his tongue into Ben's ears, left then right. They were rubbing their unbearably hard cocks against each other through their cut-offs.

But they had their rules. Soon they had to lie still to let their heartbeats slow down and then flat on their backs so the draft from the rotating fan could evaporate their sweat. Pete tried to concentrate on the portrait he was painting, to picture the maroon bellbottoms, the open paisley shirt with wide airy sleeves, and the long reddish bangs tossed over the pale face like a veil over the power of love.

Then Pete stood up, knees somewhat shaky, and took his seat at the table. Ben put out tuna sandwiches and floppy lettuce and tomato salads and plastic tumblers of his standard drink, orange Tang, into which he plopped some ice cubes.

When the soggy sandwiches were all eaten and they were picking at their salads Ben said, "I have a present for you."

In the mess that covered the rest of the table Pete saw a book-sized package wrapped in brown paper. He reached for it and began unwrapping.

"I didn't think it was fair," Ben said, "that I got to photograph you all curled up in the nude but you've never seen me out of my drawers. Well?"

It was a framed self-portrait, not only naked but semi-erect, entirely adorable, not showing off but just being Ben, happy, missing Pete, thinking of him, one hand caught in a half-conscious hello wave.

"Don't you dare show it to Jane," Ben said.

A Different Person

When Cynthia got back from her summer in Maine she found Pete entirely absorbed in his new lover. She had been living in her parents' barn painting and having her first real affair too. She made Pete take a walk with her along the river so they could compare.

"Small-town Maine men have nothing much to say," she said to give Pete an idea of the mechanic she had been sleeping with. "I painted a series of tight-lipped men. They're all really Frank, but you can't tell. I was going after his lips particularly but putting them on imaginary faces."

"But it was good?" Pete asked.

"It was exactly what it was, and now I'm a different person. Can you tell?"

Pete gave her a hug. He was surprised to discover how narrow and frail she felt. He must have only hugged her in her winter coat before. He had thought of her as bigger and stronger, but she turned out to be smaller than he was.

"Let's sit," Cynthia suggested when they strolled onto the Esplanade. They found a grassy sunny spot facing the lagoon. It was a warm September day.

"Will he ever come for a visit?" Pete asked.

"Frank's never even been to Portland. Lewiston's his biggest city. You have to understand where I come from."

"Does he write to you?"

"Not the letter writing type. Not the phoning type either. Maybe postcards. I don't have expectations, Pete. It was fine the way it was."

Where they were sitting was one of the places Pete had liked to lie out sunning and hoping to get picked up the way he used to do upriver near Harvard. One late evening last spring he had almost been robbed by two men he thought were cruising him. He had never run so fast, all the way to the footbridge. Now he hoped no one he knew would stroll by.

"I do better, I decided, staying away from artists," Cynthia said. "No wonder I always fucked up before. Frank and I have nothing in common but Maine and nookie. He's also a nice guy. That's plenty. How's sex with the redhead?"

"We're very affectionate," Pete said then feared it sounded as if he had something better than she did. "We're still adjusting," he added. "We held off practically all summer, and maybe it built up too much." Cynthia was giving him a suggestively raised eyebrow, so he said timidly, "It turns out he's very oral."

140

"Nice," she said. "See, Frank had his limits. I now realize there's a huge compatibility factor in sex. But half the fun's better than none."

Pete supposed that was true. He liked blowjobs, both ways, and sixty-nine, but they seemed more like preparation for what he loved more.

"You know, Pete, I just want to say—" Cynthia stopped herself and thought then bit her lip and went on, "I just mean having seen Ben's work he isn't doing in his art what you're doing or what I'm doing. He's technically very good. But that's what I mean. His portraits are too flattering. No wonder he's earning a living at it."

"Barely," said Pete.

"I mean I'm not going to pretend I love his work the way I love yours," Cynthia said taking hold of Pete's wrist to be sure he did not look away.

Pete shrugged his shoulders but felt his heart beating faster. He had been nice to her about Frank, but Cynthia was never nice unless she meant it. Maybe that was good because Pete could always trust her to tell him the truth.

Two Couples

When Pete ran into Dr. Abrams on the subway and told him about Ben the two of them got invited to dinner. Dr. Abrams was no longer a resident tutor. He was renting a garage apartment on the fancier side of Harvard Square.

At the top of an outdoor staircase Pete and Ben were met by a balding short man named Dennis who said he was just up from New Haven. "We trade weekends," explained Dr. Abrams stepping out of the tiny kitchen wiping his hands on a dish towel. "It inspires us to get most of our work done during the week. And this is Ben?"

"When Jordan gets a tenured position who knows what we'll do," said Dennis showing them into the living room with a familiar leather couch and chairs and bookshelves on three walls. Piano music that sounded like Chopin was playing quietly on the stereo. Pete was afraid to say he liked Chopin in case he was mistaken.

He knew he was now supposed to call Dr. Abrams by his first name. It was Jordan and Dennis. They were one couple, and Pete and Ben were the other.

"I heard your economist friend David already has tenure out west somewhere," Dr. Abrams said. Pete should have realized the homosexual tutors all knew each other. That was undoubtedly why Pete got invited up for coffee that first time. David had tipped Abrams off. It worried Pete what other subjects might arise to give Ben a bad picture of Pete. He did not want Jordan Abrams mentioning Kenneth or asking whatever happened to Charlie.

The dead face of the poet Keats hung on the wall by the bedroom door. The lips looked somehow worn. Pete imagined Dr. Abrams bending down each time he passed to kiss those lips when no one was watching.

Dennis, beside Ben on the couch, was asking about his family, his Pennsylvania hometown, and his photography. Then he turned to ask Pete, across the room, about his painting and his family and how he and Ben had met. Pete began to feel too much the center of attention, so he answered the last question briefly and then asked Dennis how he had met Jordan. When he said the name *Jordan* the image of Dr. Abrams began to fade. It was being replaced by this man of only thirty-two or -three coming out of the kitchen who was uncertain of his future.

"He was giving a paper on Shelley's 'Adonais.' I was going to the Renaissance colloquium," Dennis said, "but I'd noticed Jordan at the coffee hour and read his nametag and went to his talk instead."

Jordan began to recite:

Midst others of less note, came one frail form,
A phantom among men; companionless
As the last cloud of an expiring storm
Whose thunder is its knell...

"Now I've got him going," said Dennis.

"He asked the first question," Jordan said. "There are two kinds of questions at conferences, those that show off the questioner and those that allow the speaker to show off."

"Mine was the latter type," said Dennis.

"He might've tried to show how he was the brilliant one—which he is, by the way—but he isn't like that."

Ben was leaning back on the couch looking into his wine glass. He seemed to be enjoying himself with these men. Pete could not imagine Jordan and Dennis in bed together, but he easily pictured them chattering on to each other forever. Jordan kept zipping into the tiny kitchen to stir something then sauntering back to sit a minute and sip his wine.

Now Dennis was explaining to Ben what a nocturne was. Those two over on the couch are Jordan and Pete's new boyfriends, Pete thought. The bald one is lively and warm and makes everything sound interesting. The long haired pale-skinned one is very beautiful and quiet and shy.

Comfort

They never really moved in together. They did start using Ben's apartment as their work space and took to sleeping at Pete's. Ben had signed up for a seminar supervised by the famous photographer who invented the Zone System. Ben could not help asking why Pete never tried to study with anyone famous. "After college I didn't want the pressure," Pete explained.

"But you're good enough, Petey, you undersell yourself."

"I don't think of my art that way."

Ben gave his forehead a kiss. "But sometimes for your sake, well, at least Jane looks out for you."

The trouble was that after finishing Ben's portrait Pete had begun painting the views out the windows of Ben's Central Square apartment. There were no people in them, no earth or trees, only upper façades of commercial buildings struck by sunlight. Jane was not especially interested, but these buildings were what Pete saw from Ben's windows and it was his time to paint them. "They're like the cold ruins of a dead civilization," Jane said. "No sense of the bustle on the avenue below—"

Pete was painting a lot. He had to find out if he would spend the rest of his life doing this. Ben was working hard too. After he did portraits of Dennis and Jordan they sent other men to him, even Kenneth and Brian, who never mentioned their old times with Pete but only joked how lucky Ben was to get his hot little ass. Ben also had a session with a thirteen-year-old he called "Junior Hippie." The mother, a friend of Brian's, was so enamored of her son's cascading blond hair and op-art shirt and extraordinarily tight stretch jeans and pointy Beatle boots that Pete found it creepy. "Junior Hippie" won third prize in the *Boston Globe*'s portrait contest.

Ben and Pete worked late and never slept long enough to make up for it. They had to do everything right now and all the time, like the other artists they knew. Pete did not even go home for Christmas, and neither did Ben whose parents had said not to until he stopped thinking he was a homo. But Pete would be taking him to see Aunt Helena for New Year's.

Neither of them had ever been away from home for Christmas. Ben believed in some version of Christianity that came out as the holiday approached. He said it was depressing to be so unfestive. He went out and bought a plastic crèche and surrounded it with holly boughs. It embarrassed Pete to see it there in his own apartment on the card table, but he never said so.

They lay in Pete's new double bed on Christmas Eve and kissed and held each other. Though they had been having sex regularly for over three months Ben did not think they should on Christmas Eve. Pete did like lying in each other's arms without being expected to do anything else. It was a comfort he had been missing all these years.

The Mud of Spring

Walking home through the Fens in the mud of spring
Pete felt an old desire. He wanted just one of those disconnected hours when he could forget he was Pete and
be taken over by another thing inside him. Ben would
not understand. When Pete tried to speak of his past
adventures Ben told him he should be glad to be safely
out of that. Ben had only had intense involvements with
people he knew well though some were sad and miserable for him because in a small Pennsylvania town sucking off a friend did not necessarily make him all yours.
There must be two kinds of men, Pete thought, and I am
the other kind that does not need to love the one he is
having sex with. But there are so many of us.

On this day it was a short stocky dark man who
looked almost Peruvian. Pete went with him in his rust-
ed out '55 Chevy, the same model Russ's mom used to

drive them around in. They ended up in a drab basement apartment in a distant unknown neighborhood. The man was soft-spoken, with some sort of accent, and polite. He closed the blinds on the narrow windows high on the wall and immediately took off all his clothes. He had a brown hairless body like an Indian's and a small but rigidly erect penis. He told Pete it had been like that ever since they saw each other in the reeds. "I want to have you all afternoon," he said speeding up Pete's undressing by yanking at his jeans and then his jockeys. He rubbed Pete's bottom saying "Yes, yes" then gently pushed him down onto a reclining chair that clanked backward when Pete landed. The man tugged Pete's pants all the way off his feet bringing his sweatsocks with them. Soon he had shoved Pete's knees up, scooped Vaseline out of a ready jar beside the chair and was slipping deliciously into him. He said he could keep himself this hard for hours.

Pete had already let himself go. He was breathing in soft gasps and thinking how much he had wanted to do this, how lucky he had gotten today. It was not going to be one of those half-hearted awkward jack-off sessions in the reeds.

After a while they moved to the grubby carpet, then the man bent Pete over the kitchen table and ten minutes later flung him across the mess of bedclothes. It was not going to stop, and Pete was not going to tell Ben.

Packard Hawk

On another afternoon walking home from class Pete saw a strange-looking light blue car behind the filling station on Memorial Drive. He had to look again. It was not a Studebaker. It was the last of the Packards, a Hawk hardtop, a bastard concoction, Studebaker underneath but with tailfins trimmed in gold and a puffy protruding lower lip like a bottom-feeding fish's. Pete stood and stared.

He had only ever seen one or two Packard Hawks, probably back in eighth grade when they had just come out and he still cared about new cars. Fifty-eight was the most extreme design year of all. There were fewer traces of the simple sculptural beauties of the cars of Pete's youth. He always regretted the '58s, but now after ten years this odd automobile had become almost beautiful to him. No one he knew had ever owned a Packard. It came to Pete that he could be the first.

He stepped cautiously toward the low-slung junker wedged between a tow truck and a totaled Eldorado. Taped inside the windshield was a small card reading, "Runs OK, $300."

Pete had never owned a car, had only driven his parents'. He preferred walking and buses and subways and not having to worry about parking or traffic. Now he was feeling a desire he had left in his childhood. A thing he had only yearned for could be his. He could buy this car. Because it was not one of those models he adored as a kid, because it was such an absurd and pathetic attempt to keep the Packard alive, because so few people had ever wanted it, Pete was falling in love with its ugly mug.

The mechanic, an old Portuguese guy, waved his hands at Pete and said, "No guarantee. As is, as is." He walked over and stroked the prognathic jaw. "Fiberglass," he said. He got in and after a few tries started it up and eased it out by the pumps. "It stick way out in front, be careful," he said. He got out and patted the gold tailfin. "Mylar," he said. Pete sat in the driver's seat. "It get you where you going," said the mechanic. "Belong to dead uncle."

Soon it belonged to Pete.

Cabin

That summer they were on the road together. Ben still had doubts about the Packard, but Pete had put two hundred dollars more into it and assumed it would take them all the way to the Mississippi and back. "But you're totally unmechanical," said Ben, "and you never had a car before."

When they crossed through the Delaware Water Gap into Pennsylvania Ben called his sister on a payphone to arrange to meet the next day without their parents knowing about it. Then Pete drove on into the Poconos where they found a tourist cabin for the night.

"We've never been in a house of our own," Ben said. They lay on the double bed, Ben's head on Pete's shoulder, and figured how they could cram everything they owned into as small a space as this and live there happily forever. "Of course we'd also have to rent a studio," Ben admitted.

Pete relaxed into the pillow and thought it over. They probably could find some tiny house for sale cheap in Cambridgeport. Now that he was out of school and would be working he could afford it, but could Ben afford half a mortgage and half the rent of his Central Square studio too? Pete would not mind paying for the house. It would not even have to be as small as this cabin. Pete's parents would help out in a way Ben's could not, even if they wanted to. Pete wanted to share what he had been given in life that most people had not.

Ben's head moved from Pete's shoulder to his stomach, and now he was undoing Pete's belt. "There's something about being in our own little place that turns me on," he said. He unzipped Pete's fly and caused the swelling penis to flop out up against Pete's stomach. It got suddenly hard when Ben put it in his mouth. Pete lay there quietly the way he knew Ben liked him to. It was reassuring to look up at the bare pine boards on the ceiling. He did not have to turn his head to see each corner. Ben was taking all of him in. Ben said he liked having a short boyfriend with a surprise in his pants no one would ever suspect. It was the only part of Pete he talked about though his photographer's eye certainly looked closely at everything else too. Ben did not like the looks of the Packard. He wished Pete had bought a cheap reliable used VW Bug instead.

From the way the mattress was trembling now Pete could tell Ben had reached in his own pants and was bringing himself off without expecting Pete to help.

Sister

"This is Bethany. Bethany, this is Pete."

She was as pale and skinny as her brother with shorter redder hair and more freckles. She shook Pete's hand and then looked close at him and gave him a hug. "Thank you for being with my brother," she said. Pete saw she had baby blue love beads around her neck and a silver peace ring on each hand.

They went into a roadside restaurant and took a booth, Ben beside his sister so he could keep an arm around her and she could look across at Pete. There were two tables of retarded people on a lunch outing with their attendants. The waitress was crazily busy with them.

Bethany looked so much like Ben it confused Pete about his attractions. Those two faces, those heads of hair and freckled cheeks, those pairs of soft lips—why was he tugged toward the boy's beauty and only admiring of the girl's? If he kissed one or the other how could he sense the difference? It was not only in the eye. The painter never paints only with the eye but also from desire. Pete knew that. Once he had desired a Bathtub Nash and must have drawn it with some force of love that lay somewhere behind everything he had drawn since.

Bethany wanted to know all about Pete but mostly about his family. She could never move so far away from hers no matter how awful they were to Ben or how much they supported the war. At least she had her own phone for being a nurse's aide.

"I wish you'd come visit us when we get back," Pete said.

"I want to see Boston," Bethany said. "People seem freer there like in San Francisco. I want to see San Francisco. It's very gay too, isn't it, like Boston?"

"I don't know how gay Boston is," said Pete.

"It's gay enough," Ben said. "I mean compared to here."

"There's nothing around here," said Bethany. "I wish you two could stay."

"What can I get you?" asked the waitress with an exhausted roll of her eyes at the tables behind her. "You two twins?"

"Long lost brother and sister," said Ben. "But I'm older." He and the waitress joked the way Pete could never do with a waitress. She must have recognized from Ben's voice that he was from around there. Pete came from a place Ben and Bethany had never imagined. Ben called Pete his farmer boyfriend because Pete had not quite told him what sort of life he had actually lived in Illinois.

After lunch he said he wanted to walk a bit and let brother and sister have a private talk. "Well, maybe to evaluate you," said Ben.

Pete left them sitting in the Packard while he walked up the road to the crest of a hill. He found a stump to sit on and looked out at Pennsylvania. It was a strange landscape with long straight flat-topped ridges on either side of a narrow valley. There must be a river down in there, thought Pete, but he could not see it. Once he had innocently sketched the high Andes, but now he knew it would be too hard to draw a landscape so strange to him.

This was his old roommate Mac's state. They had lost touch. Don had written that Mac was denied his C.O. and then at his physical had tried to act crazy but they saw through it and now he was eligible. Mac might have to go to Canada, Don wrote. But a year ago when Pete had been called all he had to do was tell the Army doctor he was homosexual. The doctor asked him quietly a second time if he truly meant to say that. Pete and another young man were let go early and walked off the base together back through South Boston. They ended up at a rooming house on the back side of Beacon Hill and had sex. It did not seem fair about Mac. Maybe he was still out there beyond that ridge, or maybe he had gone away for good.

Old Friend

Pete and Russ were sitting on the screen porch on a sweaty summer day. Ben had left them to catch up on each other and gone to see what his camera could make of Pete's home town. "He's never been to a place like this," Pete told Russ. "I should've warned him."

"So you've finally figured yourself out, Dabney," Russ said. "After so many years of mystery we're all highly relieved."

Pete nodded apologetically. To him the relief was not so much that he was with Ben but that Russ knew about it and Susie did and therefore probably Marc and Wayne and everyone else.

"You don't know what you seemed like to the rest of our class," Russ said. "You were friends with everyone, but no one knew you the way they did other kids. I knew you best, but I didn't know what went on inside you. We figured it was your art. You were always there in the midst of us doing your art. True, there was Heath. Of course no one liked Heath much. You left us behind awhile there. Not really though. I mean we always knew you'd be sitting somewhere in a corner looking around at us and doodling."

"Doodling?"

"Some of it was doodling. I've saved lots of your old doodles in my files."

Russ did not look different but seemed more serious and tired out. In law school he had a new girlfriend. They planned to get married when they landed jobs. They were sure to stay in Chicago because after his four years at Rutgers Russ knew he did not much like the East.

Pete's mom came up from weeding the garden. Her pale pink bermudas were grass stained, and she had mud on her knees. The porch door slammed behind her. "It's cocktail time," she declared. "Where's Ben?"

"Making a photographic study of Pete's native habitat," said Russ. "He never saw so many big houses so far apart before."

"But not ostentatious," said Mom.

"Oh no, Mrs. Dabney," said Russ wrinkling his nose, "the old North Shore would never be ostentatious."

"Except around the golf course," she said, "which used to be a swamp, for Christ's sake. What'll you have to drink, Russ?"

In the village Ben had luckily bumped into Pete's brother John who drove him home in his VW in time for a quick gin and tonic before supper. He had never eaten a macadamia nut and was unsure of the marinated herring when it came his way.

When they were all seated in the dining room Mom looked down the table at Dad and said happily, "Well, look at me, surrounded by men." She grabbed John's hand on her right and reached for Ben's on her left. Under the table Pete put his hand on Ben's bare sweaty knee. It twitched in surprise. Then Pete caught Russ's eye across the table. Pete felt everything had come together in his life.

"I've made your favorite chicken livers, Russ. It's so good to have you back for supper again." Ben was looking uncertainly at the plates Mom was dishing up. "That gravy boat's got hollandaise for your broccoli, Ben," Mom told him. "And these are my paprika scalloped potatoes. Could you start the garlic bread going around?"

Uncle Sam

"I've tried to explain it isn't really a farm," Pete said as he drove up the gravel road to Gramma's. "Before the war Grampa raised horses, and they had gardens and the meadow and leased some pasture land to a neighboring farmer, but this wasn't a farm, we just call it the farm."

"You're my farmboy anyway," said Ben. "Don't spoil the fantasy."

The Packard lurched at the last curve. Pete slowed down. He realized he was nervous. There was Lemuel coming out of the garage in jeans and a greasy T-shirt.

"That's a crazy looking vehicle you got, Pete," he yelled. "Puts me in mind of a vacuum cleaner." He reached into the driver's window and shook Pete's hand. "And, hey, that your new pal? Howdy, I'm Lemuel."

"Ben," said Ben reaching across Pete, who looked in front of him at the pale thin hand grasped by the brown gnarly one.

Gramma was pleased they had come for the Fourth. She wished they could stay till August but understood Pete had a life of his own now. At dinner she said, "I like having two artists here. Now I'll find out how a photographer sees this place."

Ben promised to send prints. He was impressed by how lively Gramma was for nearly eighty. His own grandmother just sat and watched TV and did nothing, he said.

The next day after the parade there was a picnic on the town ballfield. Lemuel brought Gramma's aluminum chair and laid out a blanket near the speakers' platform where the vets sat. There were already a couple of vets from Vietnam. The school band was milling around eating hot dogs, and the scouts were sitting in neat rows awaiting sandwiches. Two Eagle scouts in full Indian dress could not really sit down. They wore feathers and deerskin boots and loin cloths, and Pete could see the bare skin of their thighs right up to their beaded belts.

Gramma tapped Ben's sunshiny hair and said, "I assume you're a Democrat."

"I guess," said Ben. "This'll be my first time to vote."

"Were you surprised when Johnson stepped aside?" she asked him.

"I guess," Ben said.

"It was the noble thing. I give him that. And for what he did for the poor and for civil rights. I used to think he was set to be another Roosevelt. Well, after King and now Kennedy, McCarthy's our only hope, don't you think?"

Ben was nodding, and Pete told Gramma how he had taken Ben to a McCarthy fundraiser but did not add that Jordan and Dennis were on the committee and had paid for them. It was a benefit performance of *Boys in the Band* and they wanted some young men there.

"John and his friends are planning to demonstrate at the convention," Gramma said, then lowered her voice and added, "Don't discuss politics with Lemuel, he's a Humphrey man." Lemuel was busy talking to the lady on the next blanket who ran an inn on Joliet Street with a corny art gallery in front.

They ate their sandwiches, Gramma in her chair, Pete and Ben cross-legged on the blanket listening to the speeches. Pete thought of the peace rally in Boston he made Ben go to, but they had drifted off afterwards since they could not hold hands or make out or kiss the way the straights got to at the love-in that followed.

Gramma tapped Ben's hair again and pointed up to the vets on the platform with their lunch plates. "You know, Ben," she said, "if he had better luck I'd be seeing my son Sam sitting up there. Pete's Uncle Sam. He never saw Pete because when he shipped over Paul and Rachel were still stationed in Louisiana."

"I'm sorry," Ben said.

"I wish we could see him sitting up there," Gramma said. She so seldom talked of Sam. "Lemuel was supposed to make Sammy a horseman," she said, "but he'd rather go sit in the meadow and read or play his Victrola upstairs in his room. Prokofiev, Shostakovich, nice and loud."

For the first time Pete guessed that his unknown and barely thought of uncle must have been a lot like him.

Cross Country

The old car was running dependably. Pete did most of the driving and Ben napped or at least leaned back and closed his eyes. There was nothing more to be said about Pete's family or how foreign it all felt to Ben. He wanted to get back to Cambridge and wanted Pete to leave it behind.

Their big fight was about how Pete had no idea what normal American families were like or how most people were not so safe from the outside world or got to live in some rich suburb or quiet countryside where nothing bad could happen. But what really irked Ben, he said, was that Pete had no sense of having to make it in the world. Ben had left home on his own and was determined to be a photographer and earn money and push himself and get to know the right people and not flop around like Pete. Now he understood better why Pete made him so mad sometimes. "No one ever insisted you do anything," Ben shouted over the hot air roaring through the windows as they sped along the Ohio Turnpike. "You never had to give anything up or fight for yourself. You're so passive, Petey. I could see your mother never let you get an inch out of line. You never even wanted to! She got to you from the beginning. And all that bizarre food."

"And your family?" said Pete through clenched teeth.

"I hate my family," Ben said. "Except of course Bethany. See, I can be honest about it."

"I love my family," said Pete, but he felt tears coming up into his eyes.

A Toast

Pete had managed to impress his teachers without causing them to take him up the way they took up Cynthia. They had connected her with some important women artists in New York City, and she was moving down. But Pete's drawing instructor, who had shared his appreciation of Ingres, did help him get hired to give art classes at a new community center in East Cambridge. Over one summer Pete went from being student to teacher.

Before Cynthia left town they had dinner at a classy restaurant in Back Bay to say goodbye. She did the ordering to try out her French. After the waiter brought glasses of house red she looked straight into Pete's eyes and asked, "Why did you stop doing male nudes?"

"Je ne sais pas," said Pete.

"Does it have to do with Ben?"

"Does it?"

"Je crois que oui," said Cynthia.

"Peut-être," said Pete.

"He takes men's portraits all the time."

"With their clothes on."

"Oh, an open shirt now and then," Cynthia said. "But they're all sexy, they have a soft suggestive glow inside as if the camera knows what they really want. They're very gay, even the straight ones."

"Jane loves them," said Pete. Then after he sipped and thought he added, "Maybe Ben's too close to me. I can't seem to draw other men. I can't see them the way I used to."

"Because all you see is Ben. *C'est très dommage.*"

"Well, you don't do portraits, Cynthia. You invent faces and put them in strange worlds. I love what you do. I don't know how you do it. This summer I almost couldn't even do a landscape. Now I'm supposed to teach. And Ben's showing at that fat man's hip little gallery."

"Voici la bisque," said Cynthia.

It was good and creamy, and they spooned it up and tore off chunks of warm bread from the loaf in the basket between them. Cynthia wiped her bowl clean with bread as the French do.

"Ben says I've stepped down to a smaller stage," Pete said as he too dabbed his bread at the sides of his bowl because Cynthia had. "After my brief turn in the limelight."

"That Jane is a fraud," said Cynthia. "She thinks Newbury Street is the center of the art world. Fuck her! And fuck Ben too!"

"But you're off to the real center of the art world," said Pete.

"And you won't catch me forgetting who the real artists are," Cynthia said raising her glass to him. *"Salut!"*

The Art World

They were in spoon position with Pete holding on from behind. He was telling Ben how worried his parents were about John. The Democratic convention had been scary enough, and now he was up in Madison not studying but getting involved in fulltime politics. "Are you listening?" Pete asked when Ben had said nothing for a while.

"I'm thinking about something else."

Pete squeezed him tighter. That was why Ben had rolled away to stare at the wall, to think about something else. "I'll shut up then. I just got talking," Pete said.

"Because you could tell I had things on my mind and you didn't want to hear about them."

"I couldn't tell," Pete said. "What's wrong?"

"I wish," Ben said, "we could go spend time in our separate worlds and then come here each night and fall safely asleep together."

"That's what we do."

"But you get mad at me, and I get mad at you."

Pete was holding Ben's long red-brown hair back so he could press his lips against his soft pink ear.

"If we didn't have to put up with each other's friends," Ben said.

"Friends?"

"Or people we work with."

Pete did not know what to say.

"Because," Ben went on, "when you get mad at the art world you're mostly mad at me."

"I'm not mad at the art world."

"The art scene," Ben said.

"I have a right to feel bad."

"A right to get mad?"

"Feel bad, get mad, but it's not at you," Pete said, a queasiness in his stomach.

"We're always tense about it," said Ben. "I'm afraid to tell you when anything good happens to me."

"If we completely moved in with each other finally—"

Ben had now turned so he was on his back looking up past Pete. Pete felt his own eyes must be as opaque as Ben's. Neither could see the other. Ben's body was warmer than Pete's. Ben said, "We don't have sex that often. But I do feel safe sleeping beside you. Is that why we're together?"

"Oh, Benny," said Pete.

There was something unworkable about homosexuality, he thought. The sexuality part came naturally enough to Pete but not the same way it came to Ben. Maybe we can keep trying, he told himself. He held onto the warm naked body next to him, but it gave him no answer.

Unfaithfulness

Pete loved all his classes—beginning, intermediate, advanced. His beginning students were a dozen middle-aged ladies and two retired gents. A young secretary from the court house had signed up, but when she saw the group she apologized to Pete and said she wanted to check out the meditation class instead.

Pete began with a little speech about what he might be able to teach them all and, just as important, what they might teach him. "You've already seen twice as much of life as I have," he said. "Through your eyes you can show me things I've never seen. I can help you do that, but art has to come from what you see. There's no point in trying to duplicate what I see. But I'm trained to help you see what you really see and not what you think you see." It was getting confusing, so Pete said he did not mean to lecture, so he set a blue glass vase he had bought at a yard sale in the center of the work table. His students sat on stools and stared at the vase in silence. Its shape was the same from every angle, but the fluorescent light played on the glass in different ways. No one would draw it the same.

The fall quarter was shaky, but Pete found what worked and what did not. Two of the ladies stayed on in the winter for the intermediate class, which had some younger people in it. One was the Portuguese boy Manny who lived around the corner and had recognized Pete's name on the community center's flyer. He had let the others know he already knew Pete, but after class Pete had to tell him he could not hang out because it would look like favoritism. Nonetheless Manny got him to stop in at his mother's apartment so he could show off his art teacher.

Manny's mom treated Pete like a famous artist because people bought his paintings, Manny said, for a lot of money. "Manny likes decor and styling," she said. "Manny, show him how you did up the house."

In Manny's bedroom Pete exclaimed over the drapes and the bedspread loud enough for the mom in the kitchen to hear. Manny hiked himself up on the high canopied bed and with an eye on the doorway flung his chest back and his legs apart and pumped his hips toward Pete. "You devil!" Pete whispered.

"I know we can't, but it's my dream," Manny said.

The rest of the quarter Manny was moody, sometimes eager and hard working, sometimes silent and lazy. He stayed in the studio late one evening pretending to work on something. Pete put his hand on the back of his skinny neck and said he was sorry.

"You are faithful to your boyfriend now," Manny said. "I believe in that. No one is ever faithful to me. Every time I think so I find I am so stupid to trust."

"You'll find someone," Pete said.

"I'm a great fuck," said Manny.

"You're also a nice person," said Pete.

"I'm a too nice person. It's my problem."

But when Pete heard Manny talking to the ladies in class he could tell it was not that Manny was being particularly nice but that he wanted them to pay him some attention.

Over the year Pete had been unfaithful to Ben a few more times. He dreaded the coming of spring when it would be much easier to go out and get picked up. And he dreaded Ben going to New York to take his work to a gallery. With Ben away, Pete knew he would be tempted. But then one night even before Pete gave himself another secret adventure Ben told him as they held each other in bed that he had been getting it on with the married man at the frame shop. "It shouldn't affect us, Petey. We'll still have our own sex life. And our home," he added. "But it's been happening. You understand?"

Pete could not bring himself to admit he had also had sex with other people. He would wait till Ben got back from New York and tell him about whatever happened while he was away. That would be good enough. But Pete wondered if it would be the same sleeping together now or if it would be more like having a roommate.

June Seventeenth

Pete did not like it when Ben smoked pot. Ben had never smoked when they first got together, but his photographer friends got him into it. Pete could not work when Ben played the Jimi Hendrix Experience in their studio or Sly and the Family Stone or even *Music from Big Pink*. Ben played music so loud now. Pete would never take a puff when Ben passed him a joint. Ben liked to be stoned for sex. He said, "You take poppers, Petey, when you trick, so why don't you do dope? Poppers are a much sleazier drug. Dope's mellow and cool." Pete said that must make him sleazy then, but Ben did not laugh.

It was Ben's twenty-fifth birthday. Pete would not be twenty-five for two more months. He came back from teaching his last class of the spring quarter and found Ben sitting at the card table with mud smeared on his lips and cheeks and forehead. His hair was tied up in peculiar knots. He was in Pete's old terrycloth bathrobe with a joint in his hand and his bare feet as muddy as his face. "Hey, man, am I wasted," he said.

"What happened, Ben? Aren't we going out? It's your birthday. What are you talking about?"

"Blither blither blither," said Ben.

"But it's your birthday. How stoned are you? I was going to take you out. What's going on? You're a mess."

"Blah blah blah," said Ben.

Pete felt his chest shaking. He tried not to criticize Ben about smoking despite how it upset him. It was as if Ben had left Pete somewhere behind.

"The fat man gave me some great weed," Ben said.

"They're all so pretentious over there. Why does he call himself 'the fat man'? Why doesn't he have a name?"

"Wuzza wuzza wuzza."

"Come on, stop it, Ben."

Ben slid off the folding chair onto the floor. He was slapping at the floorboards and giggling in a high register that scared Pete.

"I'm getting out of here," said Pete's trembling voice outside of himself. "Why did you have to do this on your birthday? I was going to take you out to dinner." He found himself floating down the stairs and onto Chestnut Street. There he was. He saw his Packard parked down the block. When he got in behind the wheel he stuck his key back in his jeans. But it was getting stuffy. He had to put the key in the ignition to lower the power windows. Then he sat in warm air and felt his car all around him.

He knew what scared him was Ben's willfulness. Women never scared him like that. He thought of how scared he used to be of boys when he was little. Now he wished he were straight like his brother. John had a place in the world and Pete had none. Pete's only real place now was sitting in his car. It was what he had always wanted to be inside of, his own car, his own old car. He did not want to sketch or draw or paint anything again. He wanted to sit in his car.

Ben had stepped out of their building in his tight bells and an open red shirt with beads and sandals. He was laughing. His face was clean and his hair was brushed out and shiny like a horse's mane. "It was a joke, Petey," he said when he got into the passenger seat.

Pete stared at him.

"It was a joke. I freaked you out. You thought I was a true dope fiend. I was putting you on, Pete. Happy birthday, dear Be-en," he sang.

The shaking in Pete's chest turned to tears. He knew they were tears of rage, but to Ben he had to pretend they were tears of relief. It was Ben's birthday.

Commune

Don was out of the Coast Guard and back home in Boston. He called Pete with news that Mac was on a commune in British Columbia and might never be able to come home again. Don was going out to see him in July and asked Persian Pete to go with him. They would take the Canadian National from Montreal, sitting up all the way or sleeping in the aisles. Pete mentioned his problems with Ben, and Don said it would definitely be wise to give him some space. Pete was flattered Don wanted him to come. He tried putting on a forgotten college heartiness as if nothing really mattered that much.

On the way across Canada Don made friends up and down the train. For most of Ontario and into Manitoba he went and sat with one particular girl. By day Pete stared out at forests and later in Saskatchewan at fields of mustard flower and by night curled up alone on two seats. In Saskatoon Don met another girl to spend time with. Pete had not brought his sketchbook. He had decided just for this summer not to be an artist.

The girl got off in Kamloops, British Columbia, and Don came back to sit with Pete. As they began descending to the coast Don whispered, "I had my fingers in her all night. My jockeys are so crusty I'll have to toss 'em." Pete did not feel at all horny himself. He was still too depressed.

In Vancouver they caught the ferry across to the Sechelt Peninsula. Mac was waiting at the dock on schedule. He and Don gave each other a long strong hug, and then he hugged Pete in a different way, more tender but not as long.

They drove in Mac's crappy little Saab to his cedar shake cabin at the foot of Elphinstone Mountain. "There's hundreds of miles of pine trees and bears back there and no roads," Mac said.

Pete introduced himself to a bare-breasted girl on the front porch who said, "I can tell you're from the East. You'll loosen up when you been here awhile."

But Pete never did. At the Royal Canadian Legion Hall he never danced but liked it when the band played "The City of New Orleans" or "Country Comforts." At the pub there was lots of animosity. Mac and Don played pool with the Indians and the fishermen though none of them liked hippies. Pete sat in his booth and sipped a beer.

At the commune he picked raspberries every morning and milked the goats and gathered eggs. They traded with an arts commune for fresh salmon. Pete did not get to know the artists who all had Canadian government grants to paint bright stripes up tree trunks or to sleep out in the woods on a brass bed with a soggy mattress and be afraid of bears. Mac's commune was philosophical and political. Pete listened to them talk and get mad at Don for having served under Nixon but never said much himself.

The one night Pete did not feel lonesome was when he found himself lying on a soft blanket in the moonlight beside a guy with a scraggly goatee and a deep suntan that felt like smooth leather. He had docked his sailboat by the Legion Hall and, hiking up the foothills, discovered the commune. He was hanging out there with them for a couple of days. In that evening's political discussion he had said men should stop acting like they were in charge of everything. It was funny, Pete thought, because when they ended up alone together all Pete could see was a big prick hovering over him in the moonlight. The guy wanted Pete to suck it, but he did not want anyone there to find out about it.

Mac hardly spent time alone with Pete. He was friendly but in the same way he was with everyone else on the place. Mostly he read thick serious books and had a special girlfriend who had little to say to Pete. One night when they all got drunk and rowdy on homemade screech Mac had her cut his ponytail off. To Pete he suddenly looked much younger and delicate again. Pete remembered wanting to fall asleep holding Mac but never quite imagining making love with him.

On the train trip back Pete decided to get off in Winnipeg and take the bus to Minneapolis then another down the Mississippi to Gramma's farm to be with his family.

Meadow Walk

The next summer he was back there again. In his single life he now depended especially on these visits home, and because his parents did not trust the Packard they sent him money to fly. And Mom kept offering to pay for therapy if he ever wanted it or maybe for a trip to Europe to see the art Pete had never seen.

When the family spent August together at Gramma's John usually brought a girlfriend. He never came by himself and did not see how Pete stood it alone. "Doesn't it feel like you're reverting?" he asked. "You should be spending your birthday with someone you're sleeping with."

"Don't worry, I get plenty of that in Cambridge," Pete said.

They were walking up toward the meadow as they often did after breakfast before the day got too hot.

Priscilla was still asleep in the room next to Gramma's. John would never have sex in the house but took his girlfriends on long afternoon walks into the woods for privacy. Of course Pete had gotten to share a room with Ben, but he wondered the whole time what Gramma had figured out about their relationship and was too nervous to do more than snuggle.

As he walked along with his brother he kept thinking of Ben. It was now eight months since their official breakup. Christmas had finally done it. Pete got mad when Ben put up his crèche and acted pseudo-devout about the birth of Christ when by then he was screwing around as much as Pete did. John would not understand their behavior. He and Priscilla had never cheated, at least not once they became a couple. John had girlfriends but one after the other. It was the only way it worked for him. There he was, walking a few paces ahead, probably puzzling over Pete's remark about getting plenty. Not that John would ever tell Pete it was wrong—maybe he only thought it was pointless. Pete and Ben themselves had felt almost dull when they made their final decision. It was as if they had never meant anything to each other at all. Yet Pete still thought about Ben. He almost wished Ben was down there in Gramma's house once more, like Priscilla, sleeping late while the Dabney brothers went walking up the old rutted road.

Lemuel had not yet mown the meadow. Grass and weeds stood to their waists. They followed the track cut around the edges and watched for monarchs in the milkweed.

180

"Mom's so attached to this place," John said. "I bet they'll keep it after Gramma dies even if it's technically in our names."

Pete had never thought about losing the farm, but he had begun to think about Gramma dying. She got feebler each time he visited.

"I could never live out here," John said. "I need too much activity. Cilla gets claustrophobic in the country. So is there anyone particular you're dating now, Pete?" he added as disinterestedly as he could. Pete wanted to explain that fags did not exactly date, but he only gave John a noncommittal smirk.

They had come to the path through the woods and automatically turned in. Soon they were sitting on the log bench and looking over town toward the Mississippi. Gramma had asked them to report whether the bench had rotted through yet or fallen over. The last time Lemuel had driven her around the meadow in the cart behind the tractor she had not been up for a walk but had lain on cushions with her wide-brimmed straw hat protecting her cancerous skin. What would Lemuel do when Gramma died? Lemuel had never said anything about Pete preferring men, but Gramma and he had surely speculated. Pete sensed they talked of many things she never revealed to the family.

Sitting beside Pete on the crumbly old log John must have been having entirely different thoughts because he suddenly came out with "Do you remember when you had a thing for Sal Mineo?"

"How do you remember that? What do you mean 'thing'?"

"You and Russ had a game where you were Sal Mineo and he was James Dean."

"Not exactly," said Pete.

"Strange that Russ didn't turn out homo. Last spring I saw him in the village with his fiancée. He always asks about you. Was Sal Mineo's murder a sexual thing?"

"I suppose it could've been," said Pete.

"Pete, I trust you don't walk around at night alone in Boston meeting scary guys. I don't know what you do back there, but it makes your little brother anxious."

Pete knew John would fear for him until he once more brought home a steady boyfriend. John believed you were safer in a pair, which was why he always had girlfriends and why, Pete knew, it might not be long before he married one of them.

Portraiture

Nathan made a natural subject. Pete would catch him at a perfect moment and ask him to hold still. Nathan would wait patiently not attempting to pull himself up any straighter or tighten his abdominal muscles. He would keep looking at whatever he had been looking at and with the same expression on his lips as if arrested in time and ceasing to breathe. After some minutes Pete would thank him, and he would move on to remake the bed or pull up the shades or get his carrot juice. He always remained naked when Pete slipped his cut-offs back on. Nathan never asked to see the drawings. He was only interested in the sex they had and in discussing techniques.

These afternoons were part of a complicated regimen. Nathan believed in sustaining pleasure by avoiding ejaculation. Pete could never quite manage that, but with

Nathan's guidance he did hold off as long as he could. Nathan liked to explore new methods of arousal, which for him had no visual side but was all in the touch and the timing. Because Pete could not help using his eyes Nathan had once blindfolded him so he would only feel what their bodies were doing, but now Pete had learned to close his eyes or at least pretend to. Nathan had a special vocabulary for sex. "Float," he would say. "Now a sudden beat—arch, arch! Now snap and fall." Pete had stopped finding it silly.

Perhaps his willingness to cooperate earned him the right later to tell Nathan, "Hold it. Don't move." And with Nathan in a suspended state Pete would make up for the visual deprivation of the previous two hours in bed. Nathan's cock was almost always partially hard because he never came.

Nathan insisted that Pete abstain for five full days before their sessions, but it was less the sexual and more the emotional restriction that bothered Pete. He was always left feeling disconnected even from himself.

Now as he walked the length of the city from that third floor in North Cambridge to his own Cambridgeport studio Pete tried to assess things. He knew the sketchbook under his arm had always helped him make sense of his life. He had dozens of such books, each devoted to a year or a place or a subject or a medium. So the familiar feeling of the book under his bare arm, sticky with sweat, was the place to start. His white tank-top and cut-off jeans were for Nathan, but not precisely for Nathan, who never noticed Pete's appearance, but for Pete's own sense of himself going to see Nathan. He

184

wanted to feel open, eager to be taken, no underwear, barely a shirt, sandals he could unstrap before he rang the bell so he would arrive barefoot and ready. But now on his way home Pete felt too exposed even for a Cambridge summer day of sloppy hippies and sweating shirtless joggers. He felt that his body and his art were totally separate things. His art lay out there before his eyes while his body stayed invisible inside him. The closest he got to it was when he was having sex, but when he was drawing he forgot he had a body at all.

Cubicle

The cubicles were unoccupied. It was only eight on a week night. The locker key on its elastic band tapped at his anklebone. He clutched the small brown bottle of poppers in one hand and opened the steam room door. Someone unappealing was in there, so after sitting a minute he sauntered out again and down the dark hall and around past the empty maze room and into the far hall where he heard something in the last cubicle. He peeked in at two older men standing up against the wall fucking. They glanced at him and kept at it so he could watch them in the faint blue light.

Back in the hall he saw someone turning into another cubicle, so he walked slowly by and then turned and walked back again not quite pausing at the open door but catching sight of a beckoning finger. He turned back. The man wore a blue Red Sox cap, a leather band on one wrist, a jockstrap, and tube socks with red stripes at the top. He was lying on the cot holding his own poppers bottle in one hand, the other now draped over the bulge in his jock.

Pete stepped in and latched the door behind him. In the faint light he let his towel fall from his waist. The man said, "Nice," then sat up and unsnapped the leather band from his wrist and ceremoniously snapped it tight around Pete's cock and balls. "Yeah, nice. Take a hit?" Pete showed him that he had his own. They both sniffed from their bottles, screwed the lids back on, and set them on the sticky floorboards. When the swoon began Pete let himself tumble onto the warm body that was grabbing at him and groaning into his ear, "I love you, yeah, oh man, I love you…"

Funeral

After Gramma died Lemuel stayed on to take care of the place. Mom and Dad still tried to spend one whole month there, and John sometimes brought friends from his lab out for weekends, but Pete stayed in the East and now visited his parents only at Christmas. One December he drove out in his shaky old Packard with the defroster on the blink and left it for John to deposit at the farm whenever he could round up some pals for a cross-country ski party. But despite the great distance and the passing of time every detail of the farm remained behind Pete's eyelids when he closed them and thought himself through each room, to the garage, across to the barn, up the old road to the meadow or down the bluff toward town.

Strongest of all were the visions of his last talk with Lemuel as they stood beside Gramma's grave at the cemetery by the Horse River. Of course there had been no minister, only the undertaker and the family and the few people she had cared to know in town. There was a plain stone with her name and dates next to her husband's and son's.

"It's going to be sad for you now," Pete had said to Lemuel but too softly to be heard right.

"Yes, a sad day," Lemuel said and tossed one final handful of dirt onto the coffin.

On the way back to the cars Pete lingered so he might walk beside him. "Your gramma kept me going forty-odd years," Lemuel said. "I was one of them kids that gave up early on school. I hadn't no idea what to do with my life. Then I took care of Mr. Tice's horses and lived out in the barn. All I cared about was the horses, and I looked after Sammy too. Then when Mr. Tice died and the horses got sold I moved to the room over the garage for all them years. But last year I stayed right in the house so's I could hear her if she needed me."

"Mom and Dad are very grateful," Pete said.

"Not as grateful as me, Pete," said Lemuel. "Your gramma fixed me up a good retirement whenever I get ready. And you know what, Pete fella? There's still a couple nice ladies in town I been taking care of in another way if you get my meaning. You could say I've had a damn sweet deal."

For the first time on that somber day Pete tried to laugh, and Lemuel took hold of his shoulder almost as if Pete was his son. "I ever tell you how I got out of the war, Pete? Your poor little uncle went over and got shot dead by the Germans while I was safe back here mowing hay.

I just told 'em I was queer. I didn't care what they thought of me. I knew who I really was. Maybe I should feel bad for that, but—hell!"

Pete wondered if Lemuel was trying to get him to tell how he got out of Vietnam, but they were catching up to the rest of the family so there was no time to explain.

"That's my best advice, Pete," Lemuel said in the DeSoto's front seat as they headed out of the cemetery with Mom and Dad talking to each other in the back. Lemuel leaned toward Pete and said under his breath, "Don't let anyone tell you about your own self. Understand what I'm saying?"

Therapy

Because he kept feeling lonesome, despite all the good sex, Pete finally let his parents convince him to see a psychiatrist and they would pay the bills. Dr. Macken had an idea Pete did not have to be homosexual if it did not make him happy. He did not think homosexuality was an illness, only a matter of arrested development from which Pete could, if he wanted, move on. Macken disapproved of old-fashioned doctors who said homosexuals were doomed and sick. He said Pete had been trapped in adolescence far too long. He recommended starting at twice a week. Macken had a round red foxy face and kept his golf bag standing in a corner of his West Cambridge office. He was bewhiskered and stout and would look natural in a kilt. He told Pete to think about wearing clothes more appropriate to his age. "Dress like a grown man and you'll begin to feel more like one," he said. He made lots of suggestions, but he insisted on nothing, and nothing gave him pause. He said he was willing to stick with Pete as long as it took.

For several years Pete had to keep reporting all his pick-ups and his regulars like Nathan and his nights at the baths and in the Fens, which Dr. Macken calmly called "acting out." None were substantial events in themselves, only signs of resistance to the otherwise desired growth. "But droplets wear away a stone," he said pointing to a ragged chunk of granite on his desk. "It's up to you, Mr. Dabney, to determine if you want to spend your years coming home and finding yourself emotionally alone, night after night, month after month. You deserve to find love." And he gave Pete a penetrating look of genuine concern, the same look he had while Pete made his confessions. "Women may never be as exciting to you as men, but they can love in ways men are ill-equipped for. Men and women are made differently, you see. There's a reason for it. It's not just for procreation, Mr. Dabney. It's for a more dependable, a more lasting sense of home. Vesta was the keeper of the hearth. You know your Roman deities? Ceres brought in the plenteous harvest."

And ever since Ben it had indeed been hard for Pete to imagine another male he might live with. Ben was off in New York City now. Occasionally he sent announcements of his gallery openings. But Pete still doubted it was this acting-out thing that kept him from feeling better about himself. It must be something else that Dr. Macken could never understand. Pete did not actually want to change but only wanted to want to. That was the problem.

When Macken looked at him in his intense foxy way Pete imagined him on a golf course swinging those clubs with his short arms, his round middle following through. There were men like him at the Country Club at home. Pete and Dirk used to giggle at them trailing their carts past Dirk's house.

A Crucial Point

Back in Illinois for Christmas Pete and his mom had a long talk after doing the dinner dishes. They sat at the kitchen table where Sarah once sat in the evenings humming "How Great Thou Art" as she ran a fat finger along the print in her Bible. John and Dad had gone to the new James Bond movie that Pete had no interest in. Mom took a puff from the one cigarette she allowed herself each evening and said she had been having surprising feelings about her own mother and about the farm. "It somehow doesn't matter to me the way it did when she was alive. I thought I'd want to be like Gramma and settle out there for long stretches, but every summer I find myself dreading going. It feels strange to me. I've had four years of trying to hold onto something I don't really want now. It's so empty. Listen, Pete. I hope you don't mind. Dad and I are thinking about getting our own little summer place up near Sturgeon Bay where Talcott's parents used to go. Remember? And then Lemuel could retire at last. He must be sixty by now. Last summer he told me he dreamed of stashing his stuff with his sister in South Dakota and taking off around the country while he's still spry enough. So we thought he could close up the house for the rest of this winter and maybe you boys could use it in summers. John and Cilla might spend a few weeks there with all their friends."

To Pete Mom looked tired. He could see whiter strands in her hair, sagging skin on her neck, more spots on her hands. He had not noticed till now.

"Would you mind if Dad and I made our own adjustments, Pete? I can't see worrying about that place anymore. It's so empty now. And the other thing I want to propose," she said before Pete could answer, "is wouldn't you finally like to take that trip to Europe? Think of the art you would see."

"I appreciate it, Mom, but I wouldn't want to go by myself."

Mom stubbed out her cigarette and smiled at a private thought. "But you might meet someone over there. You meet people more easily when you're traveling. Europeans are much more sophisticated than Americans about certain things. We're worried about you being stuck, Pete. Aren't you getting anywhere with Dr. Macken? You never tell us. I hope he understands you. Because you're a hard one to understand, little Pete. But how long should therapy take?"

"That's another reason not to go away," Pete said. "He says we're at a crucial point and I shouldn't back out."

"You were thinking of stopping?"

"I'm always thinking of it, Mom," Pete said sharply, but then he felt bad because she had no idea at all what he had been going through these years since Ben and was only wanting to help. Still he could not resist adding, "I come out of there every single time feeling worse about myself than when I went in."

Mom pushed her chair back from the table and looked seriously at him. "That's what so many people say," she said as if puzzling it out. "It's why I never dared do it myself. It must be rough to look honestly at yourself. I don't think I could. If you're brave enough to stick with it—"

Pete was unsure what to say in the silence. Did Mom want him to go to Europe in order to meet men? That was what it sounded like. He had never told her Dr. Macken was trying to get him to go straight. It was a relief to be away from therapy for the holiday. Pete looked up at his mother.

She took a last puff from her cigarette and said, "Well, either way I'm proud of you, Pete."

Fantasy

His new car, his new old car, was a 1955 Nash States-
man hardtop. It had headlights mounted inboard near
the grille, and on either side there were bare smooth
fenders where you expected to find the lights. This
mutant design used to send his summer camp friend
Nick into hysterics, but Pete had always defended it for
its originality. Now here was a well preserved specimen
with an immaculate three-tone paint job—mahogany
and rust red with an ivory top. The man at the Porter
Square garage wanted a thousand for it. On his way
home from Nathan's in running shorts Pete had hardly
felt a likely customer, but he could not risk losing that
car when he sensed the leap in his heart.

The tough grease-covered garage man was looking
at him funny. Pete said he would be right back, caught
the bus to get his checkbook, switched to tennis shoes,

197

and took off jogging. He was still breathless driving the Nash to the insurance broker and the Registry and dreaded returning to drop off the garage man's plates, but when he did there was only a pretty young woman at the counter doing the books. "If ya like an ovastuffed sofa ya'll love that cah," she said. "He bought it off an old lady. I neva expected he'd get a thousan' faw it." Pete understood who "he" was. He had made Pete nervous. Had the man taken him for a hippie or a faggot? The fantasy of getting laid in the back of a garage by a man like that would not, in reality, be a pleasant experience. In reality he might just beat Pete up. Would he have to tell Dr. Macken about these thoughts he hardly even let himself think? "I don't suppose ya could drop me off home on ya way," the girl said.

It meant driving her somewhere into Somerville. She joked about Pete's cushy new car and his wavy long hair and said he really did not look over thirty. She had a pixie haircut herself and narrow hips in her short tight skirt, and her tough accent came from his old boyfriend Charlie's world. "My name's Jeannie. Ya wanna come in?" She put her hand on the strap of Pete's tanktop then let it drop onto his thigh. She twiddled the hem of his shorts with a devilish smile. Pete tried to think about her boss fucking her in the back of the garage. Dr. Macken wanted him to find out what it felt like. It might be somewhat like being with Manny. She tossed her head toward her building and slunk out the passenger door. Pete followed her past a Virgin Mary in a ring of yellow day lilies and into her basement apartment.

She unbuttoned her blouse and he pulled off his tanktop. Inside his jock he felt his cock puffing up. It did not have to do with Jeannie. It must have to do with thinking about the garage man fucking someone—him, her—and with having just spent a thousand dollars because he suddenly wanted that car. So he found himself fucking Jeannie the way she wanted, and she said he was great. The whole hour he did not quite know how he was doing it, but he liked the sensation of being grabbed by warm wetness squeezing tight up and down the length of his hard-on. It was not like the little ring of Manny's asshole, which felt more like jacking off with two fingers than with your whole slippery palm. Jeannie must have assumed Pete was straight. She kept saying, "Oh, ya big hahd dick, ya big hahd dick." She told him he could come back and to call her first at the garage on Friday afternoons but never drop by because she had a boyfriend.

Driving home in the Nash Pete felt pleased on every front. It made him want to go over to the Fens that evening after dark and get fucked too. It was a good thing earlier in the day that Nathan had refused to let Pete come off. Nathan was still determined to teach him the joys of self-restraint.

The Blue Vase

Pete went to France late in the summer before his fall classes began. He took Icelandic Airlines, the cheapest way, which meant landing in Luxemburg and getting a train to Paris. Mom had wanted him also to go to London and Amsterdam and Florence and maybe even Madrid so he could study everything, but Pete said it was only certain French paintings he needed to see close up. He would rather see them over and over every day than see them once and rush on to Turner or Van Gogh or Goya. He knew he should want to go to Italy, but he recalled how in college the Renaissance had set him back because it was so monumental and remote. So he went mostly to the Jeu de Paumes. French paintings in France seemed more comfortable than French paintings exiled to Chicago and Boston and New York. They belonged here. Pete was happiest of all standing before Cézanne's *Blue Vase*.

The vase itself held an effusion—broad dark green leaves, a red and white mess of blossoms that looked somewhat like Santa Claus, and stems and stalks reaching out above. A slender golden-brown bottle, only half of it in the frame, was almost a giraffe. The lumpy apples—one yellow, two orange, or was one an orange?—the stubby gold inkpot or whatever it was, the table's edge, and maybe a window, all those imprecise shapes—the more Pete stared into them the more precise they became. They were exactly and only themselves—not Santa or a giraffe, not necessarily apples—and nothing could be more themselves than they were. They had their own geometry and architecture and shading and substance. Pete spent hours looking at that painting. It was becoming more real than his own life.

He stayed at a drab pension near the Pantheon and in the Tuileries met a student who took him up to his attic room for sex. It pleased Pete to find himself for the first time in bed with someone in a foreign city. The French boy did the same sorts of things Americans did and did not mind that Pete was older. His uncircumcised penis felt different inside Pete, as though it was moving within itself instead of rubbing directly against him. He knew it was the way nature meant it but still was glad to be an overly hygienic 1940s American. It was all in what you were used to.

And there was an Alsatian baggage handler named Lothar at the Gare du Nord who gave Pete a quick blowjob in the W. C.—otherwise Pete did not think about sex in Paris. He was alone but not unhappy. There seemed no point in getting to know someone because

201

you would only have to say goodbye soon. It was his own work and art itself that filled Pete's life now, or that was what he had told his friends at the Community Center, his acquaintances in his neighborhood, even Don when he called or Jordan when he bumped into him in Harvard Square and they asked cautiously how he was spending his time these days. That's fine, Dr. Macken always said, it's an honest basis to start building a grown-up life on, they don't need to know the other stuff. The other stuff was for Pete to work at in private, to strip away from himself and struggle with. "Start," Dr. Macken had said, "by being prouder of yourself as a painter."

Power

There was a mechanical problem with the return flight, so Icelandic announced it would put everyone up overnight. Pete was paired with a young American in line behind him, and they were bused back to a small hotel in Luxemburg's capital.

"They don't believe in twin beds over here," Bill said.

"Do you mind?" Pete asked.

"I don't mind. I'll stay on my side," Bill said with a smirk.

"I'll stay way on mine," said Pete.

In the middle of Pete's restless night Bill, who had talked a lot about his girlfriend, rolled closer to the middle of the bed and started hugging Pete. He lives in Providence, maybe he's secretly gay, Pete thought, this is a perfect way to meet a real boyfriend even if he's younger. Pete's heart beat hard against his ribs, and he could not move or dare to hug back. Bill's arm must feel his beating heart, but Bill was snoring.

In the morning when Pete woke up Bill was half dangling off the other side of the bed. He sat up with a snort. "Hope I didn't kick you," he said.

This was what Dr. Macken had tried to make clear to Pete. There was a huge distance between what Pete wished might happen and what was actually there. "Remember what you felt with that girl Jeannie," Dr. Macken had said. "You have a right to that power again, Mr. Dabney. You have gone through life thinking you have no right to put your erect penis inside a woman. But that's what men do with their penises. That's what penises are designed to do. Most women actually want them to." And now when Pete got home, through smiling whiskers Dr. Macken would be sure to tell him, "You had no power in bed with that Bill person. Bill himself was completely different from the wish you made up about him. There's no real comfort in such wishes. Our job is to keep scratching away to find why you're so unwilling to give them up. You're thirty-some years old, Mr. Dabney. But we're wearing those hopeless wishes away drop by drop." And he would tap on his emblematic ragged chunk of granite.

Pete had heard him say these things too often and was not looking forward to hearing them again.

The Stew Pot

Some local artists had founded a cooperative in an old
warehouse near the Community Center. Pete had signed
on. After eleven years he was finally moving out of his
Cambridgeport studio. His new one in East Cambridge
had tall north windows and a sleeping loft over a bath
and kitchenette. Everyone got a dozen feet of wall in the
street-level space, and each would devote six hours a
week to overseeing it. They called their gallery the Stew
Pot because its ingredients kept changing. Pete could
park the Inboard Nash by the loading dock in back of
the building where it was safer than out on the street. He
began to enjoy having more people around him, especially the women who liked to sit and have coffee and
talk, but he liked the men too.

One day he asked a sculptor named Sadowski if he
could paint him. Sadowski was definitely straight, but he

was a wiry hippie and worked in metal and got dusty and sweaty and Pete could tell he would take to the idea of being painted. Pete decided Dr. Macken had kept him from doing the paintings he really needed to paint. He had been sticking to still life too long. Pete knew that in his painting his wishes could become desires with the very power Macken talked about even though they stayed on canvas. When there are two penises involved, Pete thought, the one is the other's companion. They reassure each other. You don't even have to see them to know they're there. He was happy with his portraits of Sadowski, sparks flying about his messy hair, soldering iron glowing, bright glints off the metal, the unshaven concentrating jowls, the muscled forearms. He could not explain such happiness to Macken.

Then Pete began painting bigger canvases like Cézanne's *Bathers*, not exactly bathers but rather midnight gatherings in the Fens. They were sketchy because he wanted the bodies to seem to move around, shifting in and out of shadows.

When Cynthia came up for a visit she bought one of the darkest ones, and he also sent her back to New York with a small portrait of his dad for Aunt Helena, who came to all of Cynthia's openings and considered her one of her best artist friends. "Your dad looks like his sister," Cynthia said, "the eyebrows, the chin. You don't have his sharp chin. Maybe the arch of the eyebrows—or the soft eyes."

"He would never have posed for me," Pete said. "It's from a memory of when I'd sit in the living room with him reading the newspapers."

All sorts of pictures had been flooding Pete lately, old memories of home, memories of last night in the reeds. Cynthia was the only friend who knew both sides of Pete's life now, but they did not see each other enough. He knew everything about her life too and how frustrated and lonely she was these days despite her successes. She wanted to go back to Maine but did not feel she could leave the city.

"Aunt Helena will look after you," Pete said, but he asked her to promise not to tell his aunt about his own loneliness.

Jordan and Dennis came to the Stew Pot once. Dennis wanted one of the Fens paintings, partly to needle prissy Jordan whose excuse was that their ceilings were too low for big canvases. They were tenured now at what they called lesser institutions and lived in the suburbs. Pete had sent a flyer to Kenneth, who had long since gotten rid of Brian, but if he ever came Pete did not see him. Manny drifted in once when he was back visiting his mom. He now worked at the Liberty Tree Mall and had an older boyfriend up there the way he had always wanted.

The Bathers

When Pete meandered through the moonlit reeds on hot summer nights he saw his paintings as much as he saw the men around him. Once he thought he spotted Charlie there looking broader and stony faced with three men kneeling before him, but it probably was not Charlie. It was hard to see for sure who anyone was, and the poppers made everyone blurry. Despite therapy it was a comfort to circle through the Fens, to let his shorts slide down his legs, to feel someone warm behind him, to keep wandering until he was truly tired and full and ready for his own bed.

Then one night he got laid by two guys taking turns. They were all three bathed in sweat. Other bodies shifted about behind the reeds. While it was happening Pete felt smooth and clean and desired by the invisible eyes in the darkness. But back in his bed he was somehow unable to sleep and began to feel unaccountably afraid. It was like the time he had taken the ferry back from the Cape in a panic. The next morning he did not get out of bed. Outside the tall north windows he saw from his sleeping loft the thick gray of a muggy July day. He waited till nine then called Don at his office. They seldom saw each other now. Don had a wife and little kids and an apartment on Beacon Hill.

Pete tried to explain the strange fear he was suddenly feeling and finally heard Don's voice say, "Maybe you should go back to Persia, Pete."

"It's called Iran now, Don," Pete said.

"Hey," said Don, "come downtown for lunch and I'll give you a pep talk," then added, "So what sleazeball drug were you on last night?"

But lunch with Don did not help. The frightened feeling would not go away. Pete remembered the time Ben pretended to be stoned and Pete had left the apartment and gone to sit inside his Packard. He could picture every minute of sitting there fearing he would be alone, unloved forever. That same old car was now covered in dust and cobwebs stored away in an empty barn beside an empty house where no one was looking after it anymore. Lemuel was gone. Pete had been thinking a lot about Lemuel, the Lemuel of his childhood. He could not get him out of his head.

Still he kept going to the Fens, he kept going to the baths, and also to Dr. Macken where he always admitted at least some of his activities and received the fox's stare, which appeared more wearied now. And he continued painting versions of his bathers. His friends at the cooperative never asked questions. The way Pete cast his eyes down and held his arms close at his sides stopped them from trying to get him talking about his work. A potter named Michelle said, "Your paintings are more disturbing than I used to think they were." She meant it as a compliment. Sadowski had said the same thing about his portraits: "Pete, man, you got me looking like the mad welder from hell." Pete had smiled noncommittally as his doctor recommended he do during these years of patiently sorting through his contradictory selves.

Rest Area

One especially depressing day in August he took the Inboard Nash for a drive out of the city. He did not care where he was going. These continuing fears must mean something. He wondered if he was about to decide not to go on with Macken in the fall, if he was figuring out he had something else to do. But he was not going to run the car off the road or into a tree even though his hands were shaking. Instead he pulled into a rest area assuming it was a place to find men. He sat in the car waiting.

A few other cars pulled in and then out. Pete took his shirt off to give the next arrival the idea. He sat there bare-chested, leaning back. It was a hot enough day to go innocently shirtless, but when the breeze blew Pete's nipples tightened. He sat for a long time, his fingers tapping the door frame. He was never scared when he was hoping for sex. Thoughts of what might soon be happening set his fears aside. He must learn somehow to feel this same anticipation in the rest of his life, being this open and hopeful. But this was where he could start.

He waited alone in his car for over an hour. A cop car circled through, and Pete knew it would be back. But he sat in his Nash still waiting despite the flutter the cop car had set off in his heart. Cars out on the highway kept speeding by. Then a station wagon pulled in with a whole family, and a little boy scampered off into the woods to pee. The dad got out and asked Pete about his car—what the heck was it, it was amazing-looking, and in such good condition! Pete told him all about Nashes in the polite suburban Midwestern manner he did not get much practice in anymore, but when the family drove off he felt horribly embarrassed. He headed right back to the city.

In the morning when he looked out his studio window he did not see the roofs of East Cambridge. He saw what he wished he could see there instead—a tree-ringed meadow, a wide muddy river, an attic room with its narrow bed and chamber pot, and a barn filling up with old cars. It was the month he used to go back there.

The Reclusive Grandson

Pete would live alone on Gramma's farm. John and his wife Priscilla scarcely ever used it, and with Lemuel finally retired their parents did not like being responsible from a distance. Pete alone still needed that countryside. He had never truly painted the Eastern landscape because it had been too late for him to know it deep inside, and the people he knew there had begun fading into featureless faces he could no longer put on canvas or even sketch. The artists at the cooperative said they were sorry to see him go. They gave him a party and helped him load his work into a U-Haul trailer hitched onto his Inboard Nash.

He took it slow. He made it over the Berkshires, crossed the Hudson, skirted the Catskills, and followed Route 6 through Pennsylvania's northern counties where he thought of Ben and even of Mac, though now they were nowhere near. He had loved them both but no longer missed them. In the rolling Ohio farmland Pete began to sense something familiar. He had turned far south of the turnpike and stuck to two-lane roads that flattened out past Columbus. For a time Indiana made him sad—his Eastern life was all behind him, he might never see it again. But he crossed the Wabash and was soon in Illinois again, with his Nash, with his art. He would not go up through Chicago to see his parents but head first to the farm.

Pete's half of the trust allowed him gradually to buy John out, and by avoiding extravagances he settled down comfortably. He turned Lemuel's attic above the garage into a studio and polished up Gramma's '42 Chrysler, which had been rusting away downstairs beside the pristine '53 DeSoto. Now they were his. He moved them out to the barn beside his own '58 Packard and installed the Nash in the garage. When he first opened the driver's door of the DeSoto and slid onto its broad seat and put his hands on the smooth steering wheel he felt more at home than he had for many years. Lemuel had kept the DeSoto in good working order, and all it needed was a charge. The Chrysler required more assistance, but a mechanic from town gave it new spark plugs and a fuel pump and cleaned out its carburetor, and with a new battery it was now mobile too.

Pete took to driving his cars out to the yard or up to the meadow and angling them into or away from the sun depending on the heat of the day. He would read there or sketch or merely look out the windshield. He drew the Chrysler from the DeSoto's viewpoint and the DeSoto from the Chrysler's, or he would sit under an apple tree amid the perfume of rotting apples and draw them both together. He might pull the Packard up alongside. They formed a sequence: tight-lipped to toothy to all gums. From these sketches grew formal portraits in oil, also of the Nash, the car he took to town, with its strange face with the misplaced inboard eyes.

Pete spent his more serious time on landscapes and in his second year opened a tiny gallery next to Goran Holmberg's shop on Marquette Street. He also offered group lessons in the town hall basement to townsfolk and summer residents. People began to get some sense of the reclusive grandson who had inherited the farm up on the bluff off the Horse River road.

Shadows

In his third summer Pete purchased a forest green '51 Frazer Manhattan over in Bettendorf, Iowa. It had a pointy nose and a bright expression. It seemed to cheer up the other cars tucked into their horse stalls in the barn. Pete discovered that his car portraits sold quite well to tourists in their sixties, who might have once driven cars like these instead of only admiring them like the younger Pete.

He had whitewashed the ceiling boards of Lemuel's attic, cut out a large window at the north end, and set his easels before it. His memory of the room began to disappear into the room as it was now, but Pete would never forget the sight when he was eight of Lemuel's morning-heavy cock against the white sheets. It kept Pete good company during those first years at the farm alone. He knew it would always be with him now and was glad for that.

216

In one of those early years—he could not remember which now because they all seemed so similar and slow—Pete had driven up to Madison to see Cynthia, who was there for the opening of a women's art show she was in. Their correspondence had fallen off, so at first they were somewhat awkward with each other. Cynthia was feeling better. She was happier and had a sort of boyfriend. They sat at the terrace café by the lake and tried to reconnect. Pete had little to tell her about himself. Cynthia wished she had time to come see his farm. She could only vaguely picture him there.

"So do you think what happened," she finally asked, "was that you had an actual breakdown, Pete, when you left the East? I didn't want to call it that at the time."

Pete told her he did not know what to call it. It was more like coming to a halt. He could not have gone on having all that sex and then confessing to Dr. Macken over and over. "And maybe I've always been a recluse at heart," he told Cynthia.

"No, but you need someone," she said with her usual conviction.

Pete was not sure. He told her he had his cars for company and spent some time describing his new smiling Frazer.

Cynthia broke in: "But what is it doing to your painting?"

Pete remembered giving her question a lot of thought over the following days. He had seen how her new canvases had turned practically exuberant. She had said she didn't give a shit anymore so why not splash

217

around while she was still alive and well. She said his aunt Helena was very into her latest work.

But Pete's latest work was made up more of shadows. He had been studying the Corots and Courbets in his old art books. Those paintings made him strangely sad, suspended him in time. Or was he maybe going backward into them? Sometimes it felt as if shadows were rushing in, deepening the forest darknesses, dimming the small patches of sunlight.

Dungeon Rock

When he drove his Inboard Nash east across the state for his mother's sixty-fifth birthday party Pete took the old slow indirect routes instead of the tollway. Halfway there he met up with the broad river the Indians called the Sinnissippi and followed it upstream on a road twisting along under limestone cliffs. Around a bend he saw above the river the pale yellow ramparts of Dungeon Rock before the road slipped into a dark ravine between outcroppings. When Pete came at last to a wider stretch he turned the car around and drove back to that site of childhood pee stops, chances for him to stretch and explore and for John to stop whining about the long ride.

Sometimes they had tried climbing the sloping side of the rock or had a picnic under its brow on the river's edge. Dad would gaze into the brown water and say, "It's on its way to the Big Muddy, buddy," and Pete would

chuckle. "The Father of Waters has many daughters."
Pete would chuckle again. Then Dad would explain how
the farms they had been driving through drained all their
mud and rain into these daughter rivers, who carried it
down to their big muddy daddy. Pete worried that Dad
secretly wished he had a daughter instead of two sons.

Pete pulled the Nash into a gravel parking area. An
arrow on a post pointed him along a pressure-treated
boardwalk into the woods where he came to steps, then
more boardwalk deeper in the trees and more steps, and
at the foot of Dungeon Rock a wooden staircase clinging
to the cliff. All of this was new. He and John had only
scrambled up the lower slope and never dared think of
scaling to the top.

Pete came out above the trees and saw how much
further he had to climb, around a parapet and up a long
flight onto the summit worn flat by rain. As he climbed
he glanced down deep clefts, jagged chasms, imaginary
dungeons to hold enemies captive. He raised his dazzled
eyes from the slow moving river to farm fields on the
other side and a far green horizon. Quickly he sat himself on the smooth perch, crossed his legs, and let his
heartbeat settle. This is my home turf, he told himself,
I'm back for good, I'm not moving away again.

Once he had been a little boy down there eating
peanut butter and grape jelly sandwiches with the crusts
cut off while John was sucking on his bottle. Mom and
Dad were younger than he was now but knew everything
in the world. Pete realized now how little they must have
actually known. They had two boys to bring up. The older
never gave much trouble but was hard to understand, the

younger more troublesome but never so puzzling. Despite their worries they had let their boys turn slowly into their adult selves without much nudging. Mom said she still worried about Pete being on the farm alone but he had always been more like his gramma. That was where he got his self-sufficiency because he did not get it from his mom. She needed Dad, she needed John and Cilla nearby, she needed people to talk to or she would lose her mind.

Pete watched this huge expanse of Illinois, how the clouds shifted their shadows on woods and fields and how the river's brown depth mirrored white light back to the sky. A black hawk soared over Pete and swept on across the river hunting. Pete heard gravel crunch. The sun's heat simmered on the flat rock then with a cloud the rock was quickly cool again to Pete's palm. The muffled slam of a car door. Pete was always attentive when his eyes were seeing things. In the passing clouds for a moment he even thought he was seeing time. Time made less of a difference than it used to. The clouds passed into and between each other, but he could not tell when.

Pete's heart had slowed down. He wanted to take in everything he felt in a calm slow way and make paintings from what he had taken in and not from what he had actually seen. The horizon to the west held Gramma's farm behind it. The horizon to the east, when he had crossed the Sinnissippi and driven on, would reveal the village by the lake where he had grown up. He saw Hermes in flight, leaping between white billows, running on blue air to fetch Persephone.

Footfalls up the limestone parapet. Naturally men came to this roadside park. Perhaps they had even come in the old days. They may have caught sight of a suburban family picnicking by the river and stealthily concealed themselves in the woods. This man was dressed like a car salesman, shiny shoes and polyester slacks and a white short-sleeve shirt with a loosened gaudy tie. He fixed his eyes on Pete.

The Boys

Pete had found ways of having sex in those days of fearful rumors. They thought GRID had to do with frequency, with multiple partners, with poppers, so Pete limited himself to getting blown or letting them use their fingers in him or to jacking each other off. Later he knew how lucky he had been.

He always drove at least a county away. Dungeon Rock was too far unless he was going to or from his family, but there were forest preserves and rest areas and the wooded paths along the palisades up the Mississippi above Savanna. The urge came often enough but not as insistently as it had before, and he did not expect anything to come of it. Pete had not felt so unbothered by his desires since before he fell in love with Talcott a quarter century ago.

His cars were his loves. He tended them daily in their horse stalls. Pete drove a practical Ford pick-up into town or out on his road trips. State police might take notice of a loitering three-tone Nash, but a truck could belong to any old farmer taking an innocent leak in the woods.

Pete kept the left front stall empty in case he should find a '55 Kaiser, the beauty of his summer camp daydreams. Then came Gramma's Chrysler, older than Pete, and next the Inboard Nash. The Packard Hawk had the front stall on the right. Gramma's DeSoto came next and then the cheerful Frazer. The tractor and snowblower and lawnmower had been consigned to the lean-to because Pete wanted to devote this great dusky hall, with its swooping swallows and hay scattered in corners, solely to his cars.

There were four more empty stalls at the back, but Pete would not fill them with just any old models. It had been awkward telling Hiram Dunhill, the Chicago artist who spent summers out here on the river, that he did not want to buy his '59 Coupe de Ville. "But the car's in fabulous shape," Hiram said. "But I collect earlier vintages," said Pete. "I happen to know you have a '58 Packard," Hiram pointed out. "That's what I started with," Pete said, "before I knew what I was looking for." Of course he loved his Packard, but he could not explain to Hiram why that bottom-feeding fish of a car, the last of its line, touched him in a way a gussied up overconfident Cadillac could never do.

Pete did find a '52 Henry J right there in town behind a house trailer on the LaSalle Street extension under the levee. He paid cash to the drunk old coot's wife, who did the talking for him.

And Pete took a bus all the way to Keokuk, Iowa, to answer an ad for a '53 Hudson Jet. When the little car broke down in Burlington he had to leave it with a mechanic and hitchhike home. Goran Holmberg, who ran the Scandinavian Shop next to Pete's gallery, offered to drive him in his Volvo back to get it. Goran laughed when he saw what the fuss was about, a boxy ugly pasty undersized old Hudson. "You're the only fella I know who'd give a jalopy a home," he said. Pete joked back, "Someone has to," but Goran shot him a sharp glance and said, "Ya know, there's such a thing as a junkyard."

Dan at the Lunch Box had much the same reaction when Pete drove his Henry J through town. "I didn't know that rust heap was still on the road," said Dan. "A pair of drunks used to putt around town in it, oh, twenty, thirty years ago." Eleanor stepped out of the Hawaiian Village and gave Pete a pitying shake of her long black hair.

But Pete knew the cars gave his neighbors something to make sense of him. Those who had been up to the farm and seen them in their stalls told the others who had not. Everyone in town knew about Pete's cars. The mayor thought they might give an authentic touch to Marquette Street in the annual Heritage Week leading up to Labor Day. The police chief said he would arrange for tows and temporary permits, and Eleanor told Pete his car portraits would sell better if the originals were on display.

This was the place Pete had made for himself in his forties. Now in the fourth stall on either side of the barn the two boys, as he called them, peeked out forlornly at each other, and Pete would come and flick on the light-bulbs hanging above them and wax their finishes, squeegee their windows, polish their unassuming chrome. Henry J. Kaiser had wanted to produce a car anyone could afford, a stripped-down low-priced fix-it-yourself Model T for postwar families. The Hudson Motor Car Company had made the same mistake with its Jet. Those two little cars were far behind their times.

Uncle Pete

John and Cilla came out every August but only for a long weekend. They had Anna, named after Grandmother, and Sam, after both Cilla's dad and Pete and John's uncle, which pleased Mom. The kids liked to watch Pete paint. He let them draw with his chalks on manila pads on the floor of his studio, and after supper he set them up with fingerpaints on the kitchen table so the adults could talk uninterruptedly in the living room.

Mom and Dad always came for spring and fall visits. After Dad retired they spent the best months at Sturgeon Bay. Pete seldom made the trek up there. There was golf and sailing and a roving cocktail party, all of which his parents affected to scorn, but Pete knew they liked their new social life with more people their age.

He did coexist pleasantly with his family. They absorbed him for short spells then let him go. When he visited the house where he grew up Pete would wake to the same faded green wallpaper and the shelves holding his model cars and the Yale helmet and the old schoolbooks he had not carried with him into his grownup life. The boy who had slept every night in that room had once been lost in the high Andes of Peru. Pete could no longer imagine that. And who was the boy who had once lain in that bed rubbing against that same pillow with thoughts of Lemuel and then of Bill Rice, of James Dean, of Talcott? Pete had lately seen shaggy gray-haired Talcott at a Sturgeon Bay cocktail party. They had discussed their parents' retirements, how glad they were for them, and Talcott had asked what Pete was painting now but nothing else about his life. He told Pete he was getting back into Fifties jazz. With his kids' heavy metal slamming through the house for the last eighteen years he had forgotten how much he loved jazz. The kids were in college now. Talcott and his wife were free to travel again. Pete said he himself had become a total homebody.

Pete saw Russ regularly back in their old neighborhood. After his divorce Russ had moved into his parents' third floor. And Pete saw Susie and her husband and two girls, but an unnoticeable thin veil must have fallen between Pete's life and theirs.

It was the same when his brother came out to the farm. Pete always woke up before John and Cilla and the sleepy kids. One morning he took his coffee cup and strolled across the dewy grass to the barn. He told himself to relax about his niece and nephew leaving their little messes everywhere but could not help checking inside the cars where they had been playing.

He found tiny plastic people lined up on the Chrysler's dashboard and Anna's bright blue pigtail scrunchies and a stuffed cow of Sam's on the front seat. Pete headed toward his studio but stopped to leave his findings and his empty cup on the kitchen table. There sat John in a ratty T-shirt and boxer shorts sipping from a steaming mug. His morning head of hair was plastered flat with dried sweat on one side and sticking up funny on the other.

Pete sat across from him. In John's drowsy silence Pete arranged the plastic people behind the over-loved cow and wove the scrunchies in and out of his fingers.

"Didn't sleep much," said John.

Pete watched his saggy-eyed brother, who had always had trouble getting enough rest. It was nothing new.

"We didn't wake you? Sam wet his bed. Don't worry, I had the rubber sheet down."

"Poor guy," said Pete.

"Me or him? No, I know—him. But I didn't get back to sleep. Once I get thinking about things—well, I was wondering how you do it, living out here by yourself nearly ten years now. Anna tells her friends she has an artist uncle who teaches her to draw and he lives in the country on a farm and just paints. She figures it's a great life. You don't realize what a personage you are to her."

Pete rubbed his forehead and said, "I like being an uncle. Anna and Sam are personages to me too." But he knew there was a difference. They were not making him into who he was, but in a small way he was helping make them.

John rubbed at his eyes and yawned. Pete had wrapped Anna's scrunchies around his coffee cup, four blue stripes below the handle.

Now John was scratching his head. He took a deep slurp of coffee. "Oh well," he said, "I guess I'll get them up now. We're doing a barge ride today. You too, they'll insist."

"Good," Pete said, "I haven't been out on the river yet this summer."

"And I put the pee sheets in the washer and put on clean ones for Sam as if it never happened. He'll hardly even remember."

First Wakings

When he moved to the farm Pete had not wanted a dog because he was unsure how long he would stay out there. Then he decided he did not want a dog for fear of it substituting for his finding a person. After ten years alone he had at last begun to think about getting a dog, but then he found Wilfy, who was against any pet not in a cage because it would always be getting in the way of their sex life, and who would want a pet in a cage either?

It was surprising to wake up beside someone again, someone heftier and solid and bristly nuzzled up to Pete's softer self. Pete was still slight and compact with his angles gently rounding themselves out. Wilfy said he found him good to lean against and hold onto, to wrap his longer arms and legs about.

They took a long time over their first wakings together, letting late September breezes blow across them until the rising sun had warmed the bedsheets. They liked to fuck in the morning, quicker than the long after-supper fucks that took them all over the house and outside and up to the meadow and even into an apple tree. Morning fucks were sudden and unstoppable. That was how it had been for Wilfy in his prison years when there was never much time and none of this freedom but even more of an urge.

"I can't imagine more urge," Pete had said, but Wilfy only raised his thick eyebrows. He liked to tell Pete jail stories to turn him on. There seemed no end of them.

His years inside had taught him other things too. Until he was locked up he had never read history books or listened to classical music, but aside from sex what else did he have to do in there? The prison library had a collection of LP records donated by some old fag, Wilfy said. When he put the needle down on Tchaikovsky's *Sixth Symphony*, Wilfy said, he was caught. Right away he knew that a symphony was not the pussy music he imagined it would be but a battle of notes and chords, a struggle he did not understand but felt in his stomach. "Tears came to my eyes," he said still amazed at himself.

Pete had never cared for classical music despite Gramma playing it. The only music that meant something to him were the pop songs that stuck in his head while he drew. Now when Wilfy blasted his symphonies around the house and hummed along off-key missing the beat Pete tended to disappear to his studio above the garage.

Between landscapes and car portraits he had begun painting small canvases of him and Wilfy fucking. He

kept them stashed under Lemuel's old bed, not that anyone would perceive them as representational. They were
jagged and full of motion, colors swirling and sweeping,
what it felt like with Wilfy inside him.

One afternoon with an orchestra having it out across
the yard Pete sat on his studio floor and flipped through
old sketchbooks to remind himself of things he had always
found beautiful. There were rattletrap cars and dilapidat-
ed farmhouses and sketches of Lemuel and Gramma and
gnarled trees in muddy gulches, and there were school-
boys and college boys and young men in his city life and
men growing older and more sensual, not as languid and
elusive as the younger ones. Wilfy liked to take these
sketchbooks off by himself sometimes, or he would bring
one to bed to leaf through asking for stories—who's this
one, who's that? "Men are great," he said once, "they'll do
just about anything." Pete decided it was almost true.

His family was leery of Wilfy though they politely
claimed to like him. Pete never told them of Wilfy's
prison time or of the life that had led him there. To them
he was a country boy who had grown up near a railside
feeding station west of Chicago, had had a series of odd
jobs, and was about as old as Pete. They knew he had a
lot of brothers and sisters, none of whom he cared to see
anymore, and assumed it was their fundamentalist
Christianity that had thrown Wilfy out on his own. Mom
liked to tell Wilfy that as much as she hated fundamen-
talism he should know that every form of religion was
equally bad.

Pete closed the last sketchbook and found himself
staring up at the accumulating grays in the sky and

thinking how after this first year together there was nothing at all powerful enough to separate Wilfy from him. He stood and went to the dormer window. Wilfy was over there cursing the slopping can of white paint he was carrying up a shaky ladder to the scraped and sanded eaves of the house. He was wearing nothing but cut-off jeans slit up the sides like the seductive loincloths the cool boys used to make of their basketball shorts in eighth grade. He had taken the idea from one of Pete's dog-eared sketchbooks.

I Think We're Alone Now

There was a particular song Pete remembered from his first months with Ben—"I Think We're Alone Now" by Tommy James and the Shondells. Driving to the mall at the county seat Pete had heard it on the Oldies Hour. He heard it again in his head now despite the orchestra blaring downstairs. Thirty years ago he had applied it to him and Ben, how they would disappear together with no one else around, silent but for their beating hearts. For years Pete had not wanted to hear the song ever again. Now after all the changes in his life he could have his song back. It had not been about him and Ben at all. Ben had not really wanted to be alone with him, and Pete had not entirely wanted Ben either though he had clung to him awhile.

Wilfy was a strange person. He did not care to be much around other people. He could not trust them or even like them. He said people were cruel and stupid and selfish, but he put on a kindly face when he had to speak to them. Pete's friends in town thought Wilfy was simply shy, so Pete left it at that. But when Wilfy read a newspaper or watched the TV news he got himself all worked up. When he surfed the net on the computer Pete bought him he fell into such a furious state Pete had to go out for a walk, and when he came back to the sewing room where he once sat peacefully with Gramma on summer afternoons Wilfy would offer him the latest evidence of human idiocy. "They care more about Gennifer Flowers than poor people's health care. So he's after a little ass on the side. As if they're so fuckin' perfect. Americans are complete shits."

One day Pete calmly asked Wilfy how he ever put up with having another human being in his life. "Namely me," Pete said. Wilfy shut the screen off and turned to stare at Pete sitting in Gramma's rocker. Wilfy had not shaved that day or the one before, and his big forearms had grease stains from the cars though he had scrubbed his hands nearly raw before he sat down at the keyboard. "As for me," Pete said, "I love our life. Those people out there don't bother me. Am I too easily satisfied?"

"But you're my Pete," Wilfy said as if Pete's natural part in his life was not to mind things as much and to calm Wilfy down.

"Well, it does get tedious listening to your complaints about the entire universe," Pete said as humorously as he could. "If you didn't always complain you might forget some of that crap and be a happier man."

236

"I ain't complainin', I'm just bitchin'," Wilfy said. "As long as I can be here with you I'm happy."

Pete came to understand that Wilfy got angry in a different way from Pete, who tended not to get angry at all. He did not think he had reason to. Maybe it helped to have Wilfy sounding off for him the way it helped Wilfy to have Pete calming him down. That was what made it so good when Wilfy fucked him. Wilfy was never angry by the time they went to bed. He loved to put himself inside someone as glad to have him there as Pete was. It was not like an angry prison fuck. As for Pete he never thought anymore of going out looking for someone else.

Mom and Dad

Pete knew he had disappointed his family. He had disappointed everyone in his life but Wilfy, he realized lying in their bed piled with blankets and quilts on a cold January night. He had drifted away from his brother. He had truly unsettled Mom and Dad. They saw him giving everything to this man they would never see the appeal of.

It had been an awkward Christmas. Dad had had to listen to Wilfy ranting at Slobodan Milosevic as if he were sitting at the dinner table with them, were even perhaps some version of Dad. Wilfy's outrage sent every monstrous thing Milosevic had ever done parading across his eyeballs. He was seeing it all happen there in the Dabneys' dining room. Later Cilla, the psychologist, took Pete aside and said it was a mark of an abused child, such relentless envisioning.

Pete understood all that, but he alone knew how safe Wilfy must have felt to be able to express these things to Pete's father. Mom was not used to someone with more anger at the world than she had, but hers was a cool disdainful sort, not hot like Wilfy's. She backed away, excused herself early for a nap. She had, she apologized, recently entered her last quarter of a century and felt it.

When Pete came to look in on her she was sitting up in bed, quite amused by a paperback novel that Pete noticed was called *A Time to Be Born*. She set it down and looked at her middle-aged son standing as he used to do when he came in late from a movie and checked in with her. "I worry about you out there alone with him," she said, "when he gets so ornery."

"It passes, Mom. He's letting off steam."

"I worry about that kind of steaminess," she said. "You're not at all like that. I wish you had found someone gentler."

Pete knew it would not have worked with someone gentler, but he said, "Wilfy is the gentlest person I've ever known, Mom." Though it was true only in the most private way, he said it forcefully with no room for an answer, and for a moment he felt it was the unkindest thing he had ever said to his mother.

The Vehicles

Pete heaved at the barn door and rattled it along its rusty track. It clattered to a halt and quivered slightly. He stepped inside and flipped one switch to illuminate the Packard Hawk on the right and the new Bathtub Nash on the left in what he had once hoped would be a Kaiser's stall. The others stood further along in half darkness, nine in all with an empty stall at the far end. As soon as Wilfy had seen Pete's cars he had loved them as much as Pete did. More than anything else in Pete's life they had brought him and Wilfy together. Wilfy with his rough past had been ready to move right in.

Now he and Wilfy were edging into their fifties. This piece of land was where they would likely end up with things left pretty much as they were now. The two of them had money enough, or Pete did, and Wilfy had got over feeling that Pete's inheritance was either immoral or miraculous. He had settled in completely. He was even worse than Pete at never leaving town.

This May morning Pete set his hand on the fat fender of the Nash. When it was manufactured, when he was five, people called it "The Bathtub on Wheels" though to little Pete it had more resembled the carapace of a giant weevil. His own specimen, bought for five hundred dollars from a widow in a small town upriver, was of a pale green worn down to mere dustiness. To his touch it felt like old skin, cool in the spring air.

Pete and Wilfy did not drive the cars more than in and out of the barn and up the rutted road and around the meadow and back. Pete kept them clean and when necessary Wilfy replaced a part, but neither took any interest in proper restoration. They never entered the cars in the antique car rally at the county fair, but they still parked them along Marquette Street on Heritage Week.

In the barn's silence, as if by itself, the Nash suddenly honked its horn, which caused Pete to clutch at his chest. There sat Wilfy, shirtless in the front seat, laughing his head off.

"How'd you sneak in here?"

"I been here half an hour," said Wilfy leaning his bare arm out the window. "Ain't got no pants on neither. We ain't done it in a car since back last summer." Wilfy had a way of putting on country talk when he was horny.

Pete asked, "What, you been satisfying yourself out here in the dark?"

"Been waiting on you."

"Who said I was coming?"

"And what morning don't you come out to check on the vehicles?"

Pete loped around to the passenger side and peered in. Whether or not Wilfy had been waiting for him, all reclined in those reclining seats, he was clearly ready for him now.

Town Terror

Pete could hardly imagine Wilfy as a kid. Out to the west
of his own childhood home there had lived another boy
with older and younger brothers and sisters all crammed
with their parents into a long low Quonset hut spruced
up with green asphalt shingles outside and tan and green
linoleum all over the arched interior. Depending on who
was home up to five boys slept in one little room and
four girls in another. Mr. and Mrs. Coates took the living room—no kids allowed after bedtime. Pete had only
met Dulcie, the youngest sister, who still called Wilfy to
report disappearances, imprisonments, and deaths. Pete
wished she would visit them again, but Wilfy never asked
her to.

Wilfy seldom spoke of his upbringing and, when he
did, spared most details. He told how one time he woke
up with his older brother Edgar trying to screw his ass,

but he threw Edgar out of their bed and afterwards always put their littlest brother Arthur between them. Pete asked questions, but Wilfy would not say more. All Pete knew was that a Coates boy was expected to serve as Town Terror once his next oldest brother had moved on. When Wilfy's turn came he smashed some windows, stole food from the grocery, cut bad words into fence posts with his knife, and kept his hair greased, but after Edgar's reign Wilfy's was considered mild.

Young Wilfy did have sex with girls but knew his heart was hardly in it. Already at fifteen he was well-muscled and large and scowled to keep people away. He never did the things Pete was doing back then with other boys. Wilfy had no boys for friends, only brothers, and he told Pete he was mean to all his sisters but Dulcie. Mean to my sisters, fightin' with my brothers, scared of the parents—that was me, he said.

But from the few snapshots Wilfy kept in his top dresser drawer Pete could picture him then, the middle of nine, the strongest, the quietest, the one with insides he did not understand. In one photo Wilfy was sitting on a wooden fence along the highway by the feeding station, his thighs pressing his jeans tight as he leaned back with his butt well over the railing and his boots tucked between two slats to anchor him on his perch. Shirt off, pale skin turning red on his shoulders and forearms, black hair cropped so short his scalp was turning red too—he looked like he didn't give a fuck. The only person who might come over and speak to him, Pete decided, was oldest brother Harold, back in town for a day.

"You gonna hafta do somethin' for me," Harold might have said without looking Wilfy in the eye.

Wilfy would have made some grunt to show he heard.

"You gonna come with me to Elgin on a job."

"For who?"

"Edgar's not comin', so it's you."

"Who's the job for?"

"Who's the job for? For me. I'm your brother."

"Ask Duncan."

"He's fifteen. You're sixteen now. I'm askin' you."

Harold leaned against the fence. Neither said anything until Wilfy asked, "When we leavin'?"

"You'll know," said Harold.

That was, Pete imagined, how Wilfy started getting into real trouble. Pete and his own brother John might have been passing along that highway with their parents to spend August with Gramma. Pete might have glimpsed the bare red shoulders of a kid his age sitting on a feed lot fence and for the next few miles have displaced his usual Talcott daydreams with a more fleeting one.

"Where are you floating off to, Pete?" his mom might have asked, but he would casually have answered, "The Andes, of course," as his dad drove them across the broad Illinois farmland.

Winter Produce

Pete drove his brand new Oldsmobile into town leaving Wilfy to weedwhack and mow. The smaller canvases lay beside him on the passenger seat. The larger ones were stacked up in back all framed and ready to hang. Tourist season was on its way.

The farm road, dirt with a green grassy strip down the middle, descended the bluff's gentler slope and ended at the gravel road Pete took toward town. Even on gravel the car had a lovely smooth ride. R. E. Olds had built his first horseless carriage in the nineteenth century, and here was its progeny, by way of Dad's 1940 two-door sedan, still going strong a hundred years later.

The gravel road took a cement bridge across the meandering Horse River and met the paved county road into town. Out the passenger window Pete looked back at the steeper side of his bluff for a glimpse of that gap in the trees where he and Wilfy would sit on the bench Wilfy had rebuilt and watch the sun go down beyond the Mississippi. From up there the town looked like dozens of red and white blocks spilled from a toybox, but now Pete was gliding along past actual Victorian houses of brick or wood, modest on the outskirts but grander as he approached Marquette Street.

Barge traffic having long ago passed it by, the town's unspoiled architecture had begun attracting more painters and artisans, and innkeepers and storekeepers, and retired people from Chicago or Saint Louis who shored up front porches, painted picket fences, and revived gardens. Up on Gramma's land Pete escaped the small town entanglements Wilfy distrusted, but on his own in town he could enjoy them.

He pulled into his spot in the alley, unlocked the gallery, unloaded, and then sat on a stool by the front door to consider the bare walls until he had determined where each piece would hang. He took cleaning supplies from under the sink and sprayed the front window inside and out. He was standing on the bricks of the sidewalk wiping away winter grime when Goran Holmberg stepped out of the Scandinavian shop next door. Many a drippy April day had passed without a customer, but Goran was a reader and enjoyed his quiet.

"I'd like to see your winter produce," Goran said.

"Well, come in." Goran pulled his door shut and in a few lanky strides was inside Pete's modest gallery. "I'll be needing another jar of your lingonberry sauce," Pete said.

"Let's see your paintings first."

Pete began leaning canvases against the walls. His colors did something when they sat about the room regarding each other. On the easel in his studio they seemed moody and austere—black trees casting brownish shade, maroon sun on red gold wheat stubble, an almost pink river between banks of sandy orange—but the collective effect was of a necklace of polished stones. At this hour of morning the sunlight was falling through the glistening windowpane bringing out mysterious undertints.

"That one's a beauty," said Goran of two shadowed figures seated above an expanse of dazzling whites and yellows with dabs of pale greens and blues, which to out-of-town eyes might be a mountain range or a wave crested sea but to Pete and Wilfy, and perhaps to Goran, was a river valley struck bright in sunshine.

Anniversary

Pete knew how gladly Wilfy now let Pete do their big shopping in the mall at the county seat. Sometimes he could be coaxed down to help at the gallery and visit briefly with Goran or Dan or Eleanor, but the farm was the new prison Wilfy had cheerfully consigned himself to.

But when their anniversary rolled around Wilfy always insisted they return to what he called the scene of the crime.

"I don't quite see the point," Pete said, "of driving twenty miles upriver every July twenty-ninth, Wilfy."

"Twenty-seventh."

"Ninth," said Pete.

"Twenty-seventh was the blowjob. Twenty-ninth was the whole thing."

"Which do we celebrate?"

"The blowjob. It came first."

"I thought we celebrated the twenty-ninth."

"It's been the twenty-seventh on the calendar for five years, honey."

"All right, all right," said Pete.

"We gotta celebrate our sixth anniversary though," Wilfy said. "And then we'll go out to one of them cuisine-type restaurants in town, I promise."

"What's got into you, Wilfy?" Pete looked at the man sitting in the Windsor chair where in the old days Gramma had sat in front of her sewing machine or young Pete had knelt with his crayons and sheets of manila paper spread out on the table. Wilfy still had his clodhoppers on for mowing, and his rolled up cuffs had bits of grass sticking out of them. His thighs filled his jeans in a way that even after six years caused Pete to feel a moment of faintness, and his lack of belt was an enticement to all that came between belt loops and knees. Wilfy had obviously come right in from mowing and got on the computer and been there all afternoon blasting the stereo. His blue work shirt was encrusted with sweat and muck and hung open to his grubby T-shirt, tight at the nipples, and he had not shaved. Wilfy liked to maintain the convict look. That was how he had looked when they first met. He had been out for several years, but appearing in the woods along the palisades, lingering several times after walking by Pete until he contrived to pass him on a more secluded pathway, Wilfy had made Pete fear he was about to fall into serious danger. And then the brutal looking man had given him the sweetest blowjob he ever had, and when he found Pete was in no rush to disappear they had talked and made a plan to meet two days later because Wilfy said he thought they might want to get to know each other better.

Sign of Spring

The winter passed in darkness and cold with plenty of snow for Wilfy to shovel by hand and downed limbs to saw up and stack for next winter's fires. Pete painted and taught, and Wilfy read through Grampa Tice's history books while he played his symphonies. And when the weather changed Pete was ready to get out more even if Wilfy was not.

Lunch in town meant either the Pantry for too-dry sandwiches but wonderful cream pies or Dan's Lunch Box for Maid-Rites or tenderloins. Pete did not patronize the newer places, most of which were not yet open for the season, but when he noticed a touristy couple stepping out of the Hawaiian Village down the street he remembered Eleanor. He would have a kalua pig taco.

"You're back, you're open," he said at her door.

The nervous Chinese woman behind the counter looked up from her dishwashing and gave him a distracted "Aloha." She filled a bucket with soapy water and said, "This is not the fun part," then turned to the stove to tend to Pete's lunch.

They talked of their off seasons while Pete ate and Eleanor knelt down to scrub and wipe below the counter with her sponge and soapy pail. "How's old Wilfred?" she asked on her hands and knees.

"He's doing the first mow," Pete said.

"Is he looking for some hours this summer?"

"Not that I'm aware."

"Why doesn't he work your gallery instead of you hiring one of those Bliss daughters?"

"You know Wilfy doesn't do well down here."

"I believe a bit of town would be good for him," Eleanor said. "I only say so because I'd go nuts up on that farm alone."

"It's hard to explain Wilfy."

Eleanor had worked her way out onto the shop floor and now sat back on her bare heels and looked at Pete with some concern. He liked it when certain people in town, though they knew him in no truly intimate way, took an interest in his well being, but he also knew how to fend off advice, especially from Eleanor.

"I know I'm a nervous person," she said sponging along. "I'm a fidget and a worrywart and I can't relax. In Kahana absolutely everyone's relaxed but me. I try to slow down, but if I can't slow down in Kahana I'm not going to slow down here."

"The farm needs constant work," Pete said, "and I'm painting and giving classes, so Wilfy's pretty busy."

"Do you like your pig?"

"I've missed it. It's a sign of spring."

"My crazy life goes: summer, spring, summer, fall, summer, spring, summer, fall," Eleanor complained. "It's too short. I'm off to my Hawaiian life before I've finished with Illinois."

Their conversation had veered away from Wilfy. Those years when Pete was being a recluse he had thought a partner might finally draw him out. Not this partner, it turned out. Instead it fell on Pete to be the confident outgoing one. At first the way Wilfy took charge in bed kept him from noticing, but now Pete found comfort in being in the less physical sense the stronger. When Wilfy lifted him up with his thick arms and tumbled him into the sheets Pete felt helpless only in so far as it was a pleasurable respite from all the things he otherwise took responsibility for.

A Sermon

When they crossed the county line going north Wilfy
suddenly got jumpy. Pete kept it under forty and told
him to concentrate on the scenery. "You want to play
one of your CDs?"

"Not on our anniversary trip," Wilfy said. He was
looking hard at Pete. Then he said, "We made it through
our seventh year. That means we're safe now."

"I didn't know you were superstitious," said Pete.

"Never heard of the seven-year itch, honey? At least
it's a nice day." He had been raring to go yesterday but
had woken up anxious. It was getting harder for Wilfy to
travel far from home.

They passed through Savanna then turned off over
the railroad tracks to have lunch by the river. It was sunnier there than under the palisades where cool morning
shadows had once better suited their purposes. The sun,

high enough over the cliffs to touch this eastern bank, was sparkling off the water.

Wilfy had packed a brown bag with four tuna sandwiches and a carton of cider with napkins but no cups, so they took turns gulping. The mayonnaise had seeped into the soft bread, but the lettuce crunched crisply in the middle. Every year the river in flood shifted the contours of the bank just as after seven years Pete and Wilfy had changed also. To a young passerby they might even look like two old hoboes. "Delicious," Pete said unwrapping his second sandwich.

"Pass the cider," said Wilfy. Pete had noticed a gangly man in jeans and a black T-shirt strolling along. Now just when Wilfy was relaxing the man sat on a stack of railroad ties down the way. "That guy makes me nervous," Wilfy said. "Let's move."

"We're almost through."

"Let's move. Let's get out of here."

"Let me have another hit of cider," said Pete.

The gangly man had stood again and was now walking their way in sudden long strides. A hoarse voice called out, "Surely it's Wilfred Coates."

Wilfy looked sharply at him and said, "Bodge," and his face went steely.

The man had a satisfied smile as if he had caught the two of them doing something dirty. "I don't mean to interrupt your tryst," he said humorously.

"This is Pete," Wilfy said and added, even though the man could hear him, "I told you stories about Bodge, Pete."

Pete remembered them. Bodge was the one who always kept at least four younger inmates in his service.

Everyone knew not to mess with his stable boys, as Bodge called them.

"It's been, oh, maybe ten years," the man said sitting himself down beside them on the sparse grass.

"I recognized you," Wilfy said.

"Likewise," said Bodge. "A little older each of us. But exactly the same amount older as everybody else in the world. Ever think of it that way?"

Pete was sorry he had not moved when Wilfy wanted to, but Wilfy was handling this, no expression on his face.

"I been in the joint a few more times," said Bodge. "Hey, I got a whole new religion now."

"I don't remember your old one," said Wilfy flatly.

Bodge had a scratchy laugh, taking his time. Then he said, "Oh, I used to think God was against me. Didn't you?"

"I don't credit God for much," Wilfy said. He had an unflinching determination not to be bothered. His jumpiness had entirely vanished. This must be how Wilfy flourished in prison, Pete realized.

"And who's this?" Bodge asked thrusting a long thumb and nodding his head toward Pete.

"I told you he's Pete."

"So?" said Bodge. His examining eye stared out of a craggy face, but he was younger than either of them, maybe not even forty-five.

"Just a friend," Pete said.

"Having your little tryst by the river. Nothing wrong in that. I always stop here when I'm passing. There can be some fast action up them paths across the road."

"I thought you got religion," said Wilfy.

Bodge leaned back on long pointy elbows and laughed. "Not 'religion,'" he said with scorn. "I always had 'religion'—in quotation marks. But I got a whole new religion now. Want the sermon?"

"Not particularly."

"Then I'll give the short version, Wilfred. Now tell me this. You ready? Why do you suppose God made man with a prostate gland?"

Pete was watching Wilfy, who was neither smiling nor frowning, neither nodding nor shaking his head. Pete feared he had not masked his own nervousness.

"First you have to accept the premise that God made us all," Bodge said in his hoarse voice, "and he made man and woman different. Woman doesn't have the prostate gland, correct? So when a man fucks a woman up the ass it doesn't do all that much for her except not make her have a baby. Now the bull walrus, you will remember, gets the whole herd of females, by which I mean the toughest stud gets all the ladies."

"This is your religion, Bodge?" Wilfy asked ruefully shaking his head, which helped calm Pete down. He had been afraid there might be a fight.

"Wait, hold on, this takes explanation," Bodge said. "You follow me thus far. Now if one stud gets more than his share it leaves other studs hanging around with nothing left to fuck. But God was onto that difficulty. He came up with the prostate gland, so there'd always be someone hot to bend over for the studs. You understand that," he said to Pete, "I can tell by looking at you."

Pete made a neutral chuckle.

257

"See, he understands. The prostate gland is what makes it feel so damn sweet, right? The evangelicals say God is against us men indulging in such pleasures, but I say God would never have come up with the prostate gland if he didn't want men taking it up the butt. Women have no problem taking pleasure in each other. They got teeth to nibble clit with and fingers and tongues to stick up there while man's got something longer and thicker, see, that's capable of reaching right up to that delectable ol' prostate gland. God doesn't make trash. He put that gland there for a reason. The evangelicals will tell you he put it there for us to overcome temptation and get closer to Jesus. Fuck that shit! I say he put it there for the sake of the herd. God never meant to tie us down in pairs with two point four kids. He meant for some of us to do the bull walrus thing and let the leftover studs play around."

"So you're a Darwinian," said Pete to show he was taking Bodge seriously.

"God came before Darwin, my friend," Bodge said, and Pete nodded as if he had just learned something. Bodge was sitting up staring at Pete with some concern. "There's a delicate balance in nature," he said, "and we're in danger of fucking it up. The reason for all the crime and war and in my opinion all this fundamentalist shit everywhere is that men let themselves get tied down by what they call morality in order to cover their sweet vulnerable asses. It's time to loosen it up, men! Women can go bump pussy and have a high ol' time when the bulls tucker out, and meanwhile the leftover studs should be going after all that prostate gland out there. That's it. Amen."

258

"You still have your stable boys, Bodge?" Wilfy asked.

"Who needs stable boys? They come after me now. 'Come unto me, all ye that labor,' as the Bible says, 'and ye shall find rest unto your souls.'"

"Lucky man," Wilfy said. His eyes told Pete he did not mean it, but Bodge had reached a temporary state of grace and was not noticing. "We're heading on," Wilfy said, "but I'm glad to see you alive and well." He stuffed the napkins and the cider carton in the brown bag and held out his hand to shake Bodge's.

The man looked suddenly crestfallen but shook hands. "That your new Olds?" he asked.

"Yeah. We're heading on."

Wilfy was standing now, and so was Pete, but Bodge sat in the dry grass and said as they began walking away, "I took down your plate number, Wilfred, if I need to find you again. I know what's going on. I bet I catch your little pal here up in these woods one day with his knickers down. By the way, I'll be up there shortly if you want to come check out something very special, my friend."

Those were the last words they could hear distinctly, but Bodge was still talking.

Judgment

At the kitchen table they found themselves talking again about Bodge, who had been worrying Pete.

"He'll never show up," Wilfy reassured him. "He's a chickenshit. Only the younger ones and the stupid ones got took in. He's not gonna track us here even if he did take down our plate number. He's not gonna come jump you in the night."

"Now you're scaring me," said Pete.

"Oh, he's all lip." Wilfy reached his big hands over and held onto Pete's wrists.

"But he's the first one I've met of those people from back then," Pete said. "It was only a story before now."

"It was ten years ago. He wasn't as crazy then. Oh, but he was plenty crazy. He thought he was the world's biggest sinner. He took it out on those dumb boys of his, but they ended up liking it. You know what? I don't buy this crap about gay being a gene. If so then everybody's got it and it comes out when you need it. Comes out in the slammer. Look, it's definitely in women. What women isn't a bit lezzie?"

"You sound like a Bodge convert."

Wilfy also had some craziness in him, Pete knew, and Bodge's rant must have set him thinking. "Well, I keep reading in your *Time* magazines," he said, "about these liberals saying it's okay because God made us this way like we can't help it. What the fuck does God have to do with it?"

Pete did not believe in any form of God either, so he answered, "I'm sure the entire universe is indifferent on the question."

"So, what, now they have to make everything all right with God? What, God suddenly changes his mind? Fuck them," said Wilfy. He got up to spoon the bubbling stew over the instant mashed potatoes already on their plates. Then he took up his fork like a lecturer's pointer. "Of course they know somewhere inside their stupid sick heads it's not God really, it's them. Bodge's God, their God— God's only people's excuse." Wilfy pointed the fork at Pete as if he had been struck for the first time by a truth. "'Judge not lest ye be judged,'" he said. "People should shut the fuck up. Some day they'll be all alone in this world and a little quiet lovin' is gonna look awful good, and they ain't gonna be makin' no judgment then." Pete looked straight at the fired-up old character he had been living with for seven years. Wilfy did not seem to want an answer. He just spooned up his stew. Then after several mouthfuls he muttered, "Don't be afraid of Bodge, honey."

Pete watched from across the table. He reminded himself that Wilfy had been judged for driving a getaway car. That judgment had taken ten years out of his life, but also maybe it had given to him, in those sequestered years, something of his own he had not known he had, and it had led to their being at this table together. Pete's own sequestered years had led him here too.

Miaskovsky

Wilfy was on the computer in the study playing his music very loud. It sounded Russian to Pete, mournful and grim with a tune a miserable serf might sing in a wheat field. "It's *Symphony Number Twenty-One in F Sharp Minor* by Ni-ko-lay My-ass-kov-sky. I had to order it. It's my only one this month, I promise. He wrote twenty-seven symphonies. I'm fixin' to get 'em all."

The computer was a boon to Wilfy, who could locate anything he had ever heard of and plenty he had not without having to venture a trip to the Quad Cities where the pickings were slim anyway. He put his orders on Pete's credit card and drove the old Ford truck down the bluff to the mailbox every afternoon to see if something might have come. There were worse addictions, Pete told himself.

He sank into the upholstered rocker where Gramma used to sit and sew. She would rock there by the bay window with one eye hopefully on the hummingbird feeder, knitting or mending and playing the FM station from Chicago. Because Gramma always had music Pete had at first welcomed Wilfy's symphonies after ten years of silent hermitage, but now he said, "It makes me jittery when it's so loud."

Wilfy punched the remote to lower the volume and said with a mock snarl, "Is that better, honey?"

In the relative peace Pete was able to tell him that he had sold the portrait of the '47 Frazer, the cream-colored four-door that looked like a smooth bar of soap. It was the second old car Pete had bought since Wilfy moved in. They had gone down to Oquawka to pick it up with a hitch on the truck in case it did not run as well as advertised. The portrait was one of Pete's favorites, almost abstract in its curves and masses. He told Wilfy he was sorry to see it go, but Wilfy was barely paying attention so Pete asked what he was searching for on the computer.

"CD reviews," Wilfy said. Pete had a feeling it was something else. Wilfy had discovered the sex sites but only for looking at.

"The music's prettier when it's quieter," Pete said.

"It's beautiful both ways," said Wilfy. "Here's the sad way it ends. You better listen."

In his young days Wilfy had learned about other things than music. He had learned how to sell drugs and hold up all-night stores, and in prison he picked up more respectable skills, metal working and electronics and, of course, fucking other men, but that had come surprisingly naturally once he had the chance. It was what he had

264

been confused about all his life and at last there was an excuse not to be. To hear it from Wilfy men were always begging him for it. And through the small window in the locked library door no one in the corridor could see back to the study tables where the librarian used to suck Wilfy off while he listened over earphones to classical music and read books about war and tyranny.

Pete had closed his eyes. He rocked the rocker and followed the melody, which was running through his own head now though it belonged to Wilfy and not so much to him. It kept fading sleepily away from him.

"I found one!" Wilfy yelped from the computer. Pete snapped his eyes open. Music was still pouring out, but now it did not sound Russian. The sun was flooding the bay window. Pete had been half asleep. "A '55 Kaiser in Wisconsin. Good condition. Only sixty thousand miles on it. Twenty-five hundred bucks. Driveable. The guy's a professor. Let's get up there."

"Can you email him?" said Pete.

"So Mr. Dabney suddenly approves of email," said Wilfy.

Pete found himself too agitated to wait for a reply. The car might already be sold. He went across to his studio above the garage where he kept his car magazines. If only he had kept every *Motor Trend* from his childhood, but he had not known then how far in the past they would eventually seem. He did have the *Complete 1955 Road Tests*, battered as it was. Pete turned the familiar pages and out fell a photo he had torn raggedly from *Motor Trend* when he was eleven. It showed four Kaisers loaded on a transporter for their final voyage.

In the Ancient Mountains

Now they were among the Ancient Mountains of Wisconsin, worn down over eons from Andean heights but mountain shaped still, no mere hills. Pete had not thought to bring his sketchbook because his mind was only on the Kaiser. Wilfy wanted him to drive slowly and carefully. He had never been in any sort of mountains at all. He was following the printout but missed a sharp turn where the road snuck though a narrow gap in a limestone ridge, so Pete had to turn at a cattle crossing and head back. Wilfy kept looking out in consternation at the land rising about them. "I prefer it more level," he said. "I can deal with our bluff, but that's about all."

After the sharp turn the road turned to gravel, and it was now a matter of following the professor's emailed directions to farm roads unknown to the computer. They drove into a higher valley. Over a rise they dipped down to a predicted white house with "aubergine" shutters—eggplant, Wilfy had discovered on his CD ROM dictionary—where out front an expected hammock was hanging between two oak trees. Two small boys did not look up from their intense game of croquet on the clumpy lawn. Behind them rose one of the steeper ancient mountains grazed by a herd of Holsteins, and above on the height a forest was bursting into leaf, the sun full on it. "What is this—the Elysian Fields?" asked Pete.

"As long as they got your Kaiser," said Wilfy. "Let's get it quick and tool outta here. I don't like these so-called mountains. They keep you from seein' past 'em."

"From the top you can probably see the whole county."

"This ain't my kind of place," Wilfy said and crossed his arms.

The professor had stepped onto his front porch. They pulled up behind his Cherokee and figured the Kaiser must be in that small falling-apart barn out back.

"Peter Dabney? James Lauriston."

Pete was out of the car shaking hands with the cheerful young man, but Wilfy remained in the passenger seat. "Wilfy, come out and see the car. This is Wilfred Coates, who found you on his computer."

Wilfy was shy at introductions but shook the professor's hand and followed them toward the barn.

"She was my grandmother's," the professor was saying, "but as you see this old barn's coming down of its own free will and I'm no car buff, so the time has come to say goodbye. Our boys are disconsolate. They like to sit at the wheel and pretend they're taking a long trip."

"My brother went to U.W.," said Pete, "but I have to remind myself that was thirty years ago."

"I'm in physics," said Professor Lauriston.

"He was in biochemistry," Pete said, "and now he works for a pharmaceuticals firm in Chicago."

They had made it to the rotten barn doors, which shivered when Lauriston swung them open. Pete was greeted by a broad open mouth and wide open eyes looking up at him, each glistening with a single tear, as if of recognition, in the form of a blinker light.

"It's the very one," said Pete.

"And light blue," Wilfy noted.

They saw no rust, no scrapes, the interior was pristine. Pete was afraid he would show too much excitement. "You're sure about this?"

"I hope you find it a fair price. I don't know about old cars."

"I've got my checkbook all ready," Pete said.

"Make it twenty-four instead of twenty-five," Lauriston said. "You had to come all the way up here. I've had her tuned up and put in a full tank."

Pete was in a dream. The man was so kind and handsome, and it was such a peaceful spot with its cows and croquet-playing little boys, who would not acknowledge the imminent departure of their big beloved toy. Pete was sorry to bereave them but knew they would forget, and then years later the wondrous journeys in the small dark barn of their childhood would come back to them with a new sweetness.

Mrs. Lauriston called the men in for coffee. It turned out the old farmhouse had been completely gutted and was now filled with the accoutrements of a well designed Madison life. Pete could tell that Wilfy was uncomfortable again.

Nostalgia

If he kept his eyes off the Oldsmobile in the rearview it might be 1955 again, Pete thought, driving these country roads. He had found himself telling the Lauristons about those days. "But you don't seem all that much older than us," Emily Lauriston had said to be polite. Pete had told them how he remembered before interstates and shopping malls, before people even had televisions, and how as a child he had listened on his portable Victrola to breakable 78 r.p.m. records, shellac, not even vinyl—Carl Sandburg singing "The Foggy Foggy Dew" and Burl Ives "The Bold Soldier." Now in the Kaiser these songs were coming back to his ears while Wilfy in the car behind was no doubt groaning his own strange version of a Russian symphony.

Pete wished he could hear his old records again. They had still been in his closet when he went off to

Harvard, but then his mom took them to the rummage sale just as he would later pitilessly sell off his Everly Brothers and Buddy Holly 45s at a hippie flea market in Cambridge. You never know when to keep things, he thought. He yearned not only to hear the songs again but to hold the scratched-up records in his hands, to watch their labels spinning around so fast and hear that tinny speaker encased in brown Bakelite singing out to him. He wanted to see those albums—Carl Sandburg looking glum, a wry smile on Burl Ives. But as Pete drove on through unknown Wisconsin on his way home with Wilfy somewhere behind he decided that with his Kaiser he had perhaps retrieved as much as he still needed. Back then he had only seen this rare creature parked in front of someone's house but gone the next day or passing on the road in the opposite direction like a vision. Now he could rest his eyes on its every line. He wondered if his paintings might surprise him this year. His talk with the Lauristons had told him he was looking back in a new way. It all belonged to him now. "When I was little there were thousands of people still alive who had been born into slavery," he had told them. "I was much closer to the nineteenth century than I am now to my own child-hood. We were all afraid of polio. We were quarantined with a 'Q' on the door when my brother John got scarlet fever."

"I'm sorry our boys are being so diffident about their great-grandmother's car," Emily said. "They're usually friendlier."

Wilfy was drumming his fingers on their kitchen table, which looked like a giant bread board.

271

"I understand their feelings," Pete said.

"Well, we're glad the old buggy's found a good home," said the professor, who since they had come inside had been letting his wife do most of the talking.

Now on the road Pete checked in the rearview for the Olds. They were both soon out on the main highway again going south and back into 1999 where the pale blue car Pete was driving was more of an artifact than a conveyance. Tomorrow he would begin a new series of portraits.

When Pete approached the old barn, its door hanging open to receive the Kaiser, he drove very slowly to the back and swung into the only empty stall. Wilfy pulled the Olds up in the yard and yelled over his music, "You should've backed in so it faces out like the others."

"I wanted to make sure I could make the turn," Pete called out from the dark. It was just as Wherry's book said: the car had precise handling. But Pete did not want to look over his treasure too closely. He would wait till morning light.

Large River Scene

Hiram Dunhill, the best known artist in town, had opened for the 2001 season. He had been cordial two decades ago when Pete started his own gallery. Despite having a wife Hiram was surely gay. He had a lakefront studio in Chicago and in winter only came out to judge the county arts competition. Pete had won a grant his first year living at the farm but had never been asked to serve on the committee, and when a decent three years later he applied again for a grant he had been awarded nothing, so he never tried again. Hiram continued to be pleasant when they met on Marquette Street.

The townsfolk who took classes from Pete rated Hiram Dunhill far beyond their small aspirations. They saw Pete—no Chicago artist—as an unintimidating amateur with enough technique to be a good teacher, but Dunhill painted the way they expected a painter to paint.

Peter Dabney painted quirkily, not the sort of thing they would want above their mantelpieces except maybe a car portrait for their den. They were polite about his work but preferred him concentrating on their own paintings.

Pete stuck his head in Hiram's open door. A slim young man in black jeans and a red T-shirt was arranging the track lighting from a stepladder. Hiram swept in from the back room saying, "Ah, Peter, good to see you, this is Barry. Barry, this is Peter Dabney from the little gallery down the block. He's a marvelous painter. How were your ladies this winter?"

"And a few gentlemen," Pete said. "We had a good time."

"It's going to be a grim summer—high gas prices, economy shaky," Hiram said steadying Barry's ladder for him. "But another school of thought says it'll keep people closer to home, so we may get the suburban crowd that usually flies farther afield. Barry will be helping me out. Have you got someone?"

"Winslow Bliss, I hope."

"They pass as in a stream, the Bliss girls," Hiram remarked. "Winnie's a peach."

"This is handsome," Pete said of a very large river scene dominating the far wall to which Barry was trying to direct the most effective lighting—barges tied up at a wharf, boys scrambling about unloading bales, ladies in long skirts passing with scarcely a glance, all in a shimmering summer haze.

"Oh, it won't sell, but the larger works draw them in," Hiram said. "I hope I have something left for Heritage Week. You bringing your cars down?" Barry stepped off the ladder and bumped into Hiram who gracefully moved aside but placed a hand on Barry's narrow shoulder as they assessed the lighting. "Peter has marvelous old cars," he explained. "Among other talents he's an automotive portraitist. People do love his cars. I aim at dimmer nostalgias because Peter has a corner on the 1950s."

Pete felt he had to say, "I'm not particularly nostalgic. I like the shapes."

"I'm sorry I'm so busy," Hiram said abruptly.

"I just stopped to welcome you back," said Pete. "But I'll be by again."

"And how's Wilfred?" Hiram asked then said aside to Barry, "That's Peter's friend."

"He's well," said Pete at the door.

Hiram smiled but had nothing more to say. His eyes began darting about the large room, calculating. Barry had posed himself against the stepladder, one hand on the bare hipbone jutting up between his low-slung jeans and his riding up red T-shirt. With his other hand he waved a somewhat ambiguous goodbye.

Live With It

Later in the day Wilfy drove down to meet Pete at the gallery. Pete was mulling over his new price list. He had no prices in mind while he painted. He did not even have buyers in mind. He painted as if he would keep each painting for himself and live with it forever over the fireplace or the sideboard. That was the only way he could work.

But he drew almost so that he could rip the drawings out of his sketchbook and give them to someone or else store them away for years unlooked at. Wilfy felt Pete should sell his drawings too, but then he would not be able to draw them as freely. Wilfy also felt Pete underpriced his paintings because he had no sure sense of their value. Tourists took local artists at their own estimation, Wilfy claimed, so Hiram Dunhill's work came quickly in and out while Pete's stayed there week after week. But Pete was glad to live that much longer with his.

Now Wilfy was going over the price list, but he had stopped suggesting Pete hike it up thirty percent. "I'd rather not have anyone feel taken advantage of," Pete said waiting for Wilfy's approval.

"Now it'll about pay the gallery rent," Wilfy said.

"And I have to pay Winslow," said Pete.

"You've got a summer ahead. Do more cars. Heritage Week folks like 'em. But the money's not the point," said Wilfy to Pete's surprise. "It's sending your pictures out in the world."

"Says he who never leaves home."

"But the deal is," Wilfy added solemnly, "you and me stay home, and your pictures go out instead of us. I like thinking of them out there." Then Wilfy's eyes seemed to focus on something far away. For a time he was lost in one of his philosophical speculations. Then he said, "But eventually everything out there will totally disappear, so who gives a flying fuck!"

His Small Self

Wilfy had pulled the Kaiser into the yard for its annual tune-up. He got to each of the cars one by one through the summer. From his studio window Pete watched him leaning under the raised hood, which was light blue as the sky with a sharp glinting spot where the sun struck it. He would have to do a portrait from that angle.

Pete knew nothing about the inner workings of his cars. When he was young he and his friend Nick at summer camp had memorized statistics from their magazines as if they meant something though neither boy had yet been behind the wheel of anything larger than a carnival Dodgem. All Nick could talk about their second summer was the new line Ford had under development. "This much is certain," he told Pete, "the Ford Motor Company cannot design a bad car. That's the kind of faith I have in them." By the time the Edsel appeared with its oddly surprised expression Nick and Pete were back to their separate school years and never wrote each other though Pete kept thinking they might. Nick was my best friend for two summers, he used to tell himself, but now it's completely over. And as he watched Wilfy slide on his back under the last of the Kaisers he wondered if a fifty-six-year-old Nick somewhere had any memory at all of the boy he had once talked cars with or any memory of that night Bruce with his standing up boner had crossed the cabin floor toward Nelson's bare bottom. Where are those two boys at fifty-six? Most likely grandfathers. Am I the only person on earth who still envisions that one summer night?

Nick had always tolerated Pete's love of Kaisers and Frazers. He had even found in the magazine bin at the camp mess hall an old *National Geographic* with a '51 Frazer ad and risked being caught ripping it out for Pete. He called Pete "Kaiser Frazer" or sometimes "Supercharger," which Pete liked better. In the woods when no other campers were around they pretended to be a Thunderbird and a Kaiser Darrin running down the paths roaring and screeching, accelerating and braking. It was Nick's idea, but Pete joined in even though he preferred lying on their bunks and drawing their favorite models. He remembered all this as if he still might find his small self running about the woods of the Upper Peninsula.

For some time Pete's eyes had been contemplating that light blue automobile reposing in the sun down there, so familiar from his dreams but never his until now. Wilfy was under the chassis with his ragged blue jeans and muddy boots sticking out.

On the Couch

In the cold months in the evenings Wilfy and Pete stuck to the kitchen and sewing room, but now in late June with the windows open again they favored the living room along the shady side of the house. After dinner they came and sat on the couch, Wilfy's gray socks up on the coffee table, Pete leaning into his shoulder, a hand on Wilfy's thigh and Wilfy's arm down along Pete's back. Light was filling the sun porch behind the French doors, but in here it was shadowy and restful. Pete shut his eyes so he could not see Wilfy's jeans but only feel their worn softness and smell the grass stains and his sweat.

After some silence Wilfy said, "I ordered a couple more CDs today, just so you know."

"Finding more Miaskovskys?"

"And this other Commie by the name of Kabalev-sky."

"You love your Russians, Wilfy."

"I have Kabalevsky's *First* and *Second*, and I've ordered the *Fourth*, but they haven't recorded the *Third*. It bugs me."

"Do you love the Russians because they used to be the enemy?"

"Not my enemy, boy," said Wilfy. "Besides they were our allies in World War One and World War Two. You don't know much about the past, Pete."

Pete was content to let Wilfy have the final word on history. It helped even them out.

"I been movin' along on your grampa's shelf of World War One books. This afternoon I was out under the tree readin' *The Outbreak of War* by E. F. Benson. Do you realize the whole thing was a stupid fuck up? People are assholes. They ask for all the crap they get."

"But you love your grim symphonies about suffering and death."

"Not only about suffering and death, honey. What about Proko-feef's *Fifth Symphony in B flat major*? I'm going to make you listen to it. He wrote it the summer you were born, 1944. It's exactly as old as you. It's in honor of the Commies smashin' the Nazis."

"How do you know these things?"

"I read the little booklets. Everything I know I learn from readin' it in books. How else would I know it?"

"Wilfy," said Pete running his fingers along the smelly old jeans.

"We're going to listen to it together," Wilfy announced. "You never listen to whole symphonies with me. Last time I listened to a whole symphony with someone it was probably back in the pen with my buddy the librarian down there under the table lickin' my balls."

"You and your jail stories, Wilfy. I don't know who was worse in there, you or that Bodge."

"You still frettin' about Bodge? Couldn't you see he's a big chickenshit? Besides he only went for scum. I got the pretty ones. And you think my stories are bad! What about you and *your* stories? You been way worse than I ever been."

"I got an earlier start," said Pete.

"Way worse." Wilfy snorted and leaned back pulling Pete along with him up to his chest. "But whose fuckin' business is it anyway? One person's worse is another's hot time."

The light in the French doors had dimmed to purple. It was the beginning of an evening when neither of them was thinking of having sex. Twice a week was usually plenty now, and Pete did not even mind the prospect of once a week. They had their separate pursuits, but together they had talks like this one and cooked their country meals and fixed up their creaky house and cared for their quiet land. They had their old cars and a Ford truck and a serviceable Oldsmobile. They had their slow walks and at night their falling asleep together in one bed. They had it for now. When they were both gone it would be up to young Anna and Sam Dabney to decide what to do with what was left.

The Twentieth Century

In the summer doldrums Russ drove out to see Pete, his oldest friend. He wanted to buy a painting for his bride to be. "It's a low-key second wedding for each of us," he had said on the phone, "but I want something for her that's one of a kind."

Now they were standing in Pete's sticky hot studio with the window fan barely creating a breeze. Pete had set some recent landscapes one by one on the bigger easel. Russ considered each with a nod or a tilt of his graying head, his lips in an uncertain half smile. "Or a still life?" Pete asked with Russ still looking unsatisfied. "I do still life mostly in the winter, but I've got a few old ones here. Lots of neat stuff to work with," he said pointing to Gramma's pitchers and bowls and vases on the corner shelves. "And I like wormy apples and gourds and Indian corn." He drew some canvases from the wall rack and set each one on the easel. Russ watched in silence. The last was of blue and green glass bottles along a windowsill with bare trees outside.

"So that's the tail end of twentieth-century painting," Russ declared. "Remember in school they were always talking about twentieth-century art and twentieth-century music and twentieth-century poetry like it was totally modern and difficult and was changing the way we thought about life? I used to get so excited. I expected everything to go on getting weirder and weirder, but it never did."

Pete put up a small canvas of eggs in a wooden bowl. "At the time I didn't really think about it," he said. "You were the thinker."

"It's arbitrary anyway, centuries," said Russ. "Who says one hundred is a magic number?"

"I miss the twentieth century now," Pete said thinking only of the parts that had been beautiful.

Russ had turned his attention to the stack of car portraits leaning against the wall. "I don't think she'd want one of these," he said. "Kate's more the old-fashioned avant-garde sort like me. I mean I like all your stuff, Pete, very much, but don't you have anything more unsettling?"

Pete had to mull it over before he decided to reach under the day bed for the secret paintings he had done when he and Wilfy first got together. "Here's some earlier stuff," he said. "It's not what I'd show in town." He set the canvases one at a time on the smaller easel.

Russ looked closely, lifting and lowering his chin to account for his bifocals. "There's something sexual about them," he said.

"You would see that," said Pete with a sly smile that did not let Russ know he was right.

"But, I mean, look at the way this huge dark cloud or whatever it is—I mean, everything's shaking."

Pete was pleased but did not say so.

"Of course there's something sexual about those gourds over there too," Russ said.

Pete watched Russ picking up and studying each of the secret canvases. His tall self was as skinny as ever but his skin was papery now, and looking closer with his artist's eyes Pete saw the tiny lines of age that made Russ into an older man. Pete cast his eyes to the floorboards and then tried glancing up to one side to catch a blurrier sense of the Russ he remembered. Russ had his hands on his narrow hips, and his skinny elbows were sticking out. He was carefully inspecting each of the dark swirling little paintings Pete had never even shown to Wilfy.

Russ finally said, "How much for these two? I like them as a pair."

"They're your wedding present," said Pete.

So they took the two paintings Russ had chosen and sat on the day bed in the breeze from the fan each holding one. Pete knew they saw different things in those dark swirls.

"Remember Catullus?" Russ asked. "'O! your protruding nipples! *Mea manus est cupida!*' Remember?"

Pete nodded.

"I was such a creepy kid in eighth grade," Russ said. "What did you think of me?"

"You made me feel less strange about myself," Pete said.

"That's something."

"You were my only real friend. You weren't creepy, Russ. I mean, how do young kids ever figure out sex?"

"How does anybody ever?"

They sat side by side with the little paintings on their laps. It was like being in Russ's old room with his files of clippings and his Orff records and his James Dean photo on the wall.

"Are you truly all right, Pete?" Russ asked. "You're being safe, you and Wilfy? Many times over the years I've wondered if I'd even find you still alive."

"We've been lucky," said Pete.

Russ nodded and traded canvases with Pete so he could stare into the other one to see what he could find there.

Pete began thinking about a statue he had seen in Paris of a boyish Mercury crawling naked along the ground, fascinated, twisting live snakes about his wand, inventing the caduceus. Pete looked down at the wedding present he now held. It showed no such supple thighs or beautifully round buttocks, no muscular arms outstretched, but there was something else there Pete could not quite see no matter how closely he tried to peer into the dark paint, something not at all ugly. Pete did not understand his own work. Might he be seeing himself inside it?

Heritage

At the end of August a letter came to Pete from Lemuel's sister in South Dakota saying her brother had died out west at the age of eighty-six and she had informed Mrs. Tice's executor to stop sending the checks. Pete called Mom up in Sturgeon Bay. She was more upset than he expected. It was cocktail hour, and Dad was not back yet from his golf.

This was the week Pete and Wilfy were polishing the cars to be ready to trundle them down to Marquette Street for Heritage Week. The police chief had delivered ten temporary permits to tape to the windshields, and Wilfy had put enough gas in each tank to make it down the bluff and back up again. As usual Wilfy was nervous about the cars being gone for a whole week, parked down there in public where anyone could vandalize them. He proposed he and Pete trade off keeping watch from the gallery, but Pete reminded him that nothing bad had ever happened in all the years they had taken part. It was a safe sleepy town of trustworthy citizens and tourists who bought art and country crafts and stayed at bed and breakfasts, for Christ's sake. Wilfy said he could not trust any American now that George W. Bush was president. "You'll see what this country's really made of," he told Pete.

Wilfy had been cranky ever since Pete's fifty-seventh birthday when they had to put off listening to Prokofiev's *Fifth* because John and Cilla had come out with the kids. And Wilfy had figured that something had gone on between Pete and his brother that Pete would not tell him. After John and his family left Pete could not entirely mask his glum mood but tried to pass it off as residual brotherly tension.

In fact John and Pete had gone off for one of their morning walks because John had said he had some things on his mind he wanted to talk about. Cilla had recommended it.

"What is it?" Pete asked feeling slightly fearful as they set out.

"Oh, I don't know," John said, "I suppose it's mostly my problem. It's different being the younger brother. I'm always comparing myself. You never compared yourself to me or anyone. You were just Pete. I had to go around figuring everything out on my own."

They were trudging up the rutted road. Pete looked closely at John, who was wiping sweat from his forehead and not looking at him. They did not say anything more until they reached the top of the hill where Pete stopped and said, "Let's sit here in the shade, John. I'm sorry my life has been so different from yours. Is it about Wilfy?"

John sat down cross-legged in the dry grass. Pete stretched out beside him, the grass tickling his legs. "Wilfy doesn't bother me anymore," John said. "I'm used to him. But I was originally the unconventional one. It's more likely I would've known a Wilfy type back then. I don't understand how I got so cautious and you get to keep doing whatever you want."

Pete had known this feeling was there inside John waiting to come out. His face was struggling with how to put it. Pete touched his brother's elbow the way he might have back when he told him bedtime stories.

"I'm not saying I didn't want you to buy me out of the farm," John said. "I'm not saying you shouldn't have given up on your career in Cambridge. But I love your paintings, I love the ones we have hanging in our house, I'm proud of them, I show them to all our friends. I explain that you're too modest, you should be better known."

"I'm not good at pushing myself," Pete conceded.

"No, but you get to spend your whole life anyway doing what you love. Not that I don't love doing my research, I mean for its own sake, but somehow I'm so bourgeois."

In the apple tree's shade the drops of sweat were evaporating from John's brow. He ran the back of his hand across it and wiped the last dampness onto his T-shirt. Pete did not know what he could say, so he waited.

Finally John said, "I suppose I've been thinking a lot about myself when we were kids. And," he said reluctantly, "how you let me down. Oh, boogers! I'm sorry, Pete."

Pete was thinking about it. Then he prompted, "By not being a normal older brother?"

John seemed to think that was it. He was slowly, slowly nodding his whole head as if he might cry. Pete held onto John's sweaty knee and put his other arm across his damp T-shirt. A few tears finally joined the sweat on John's cheeks. "Funny thing about being normal," he said, "maybe it's not such a good deal. Of course, Dad likes me being normal. He even still thinks you could've been. We were having a talk about you on the phone last week. He was asking me why you couldn't have found another fellow like Ben or some gay version of Russ. There's plenty of normal gay couples these days, he was telling me."

Pete pulled his arms back, wrapped them around his bare knees, and managed to chuckle.

"You got away with it because of your painting," John said. "Where did your painting come from? Cilla says it's deep in your psychology, that everything has to start somewhere."

"I don't know where my painting came from," said Pete squinting into the sun. "I saw other people's faces, their bodies, more clearly than my own. I could stare for a whole hour at a tree or a car. I probably spent too much time watching things from a distance. I'm sorry, John."

"I always wanted you to teach me," John said. "I don't remember you ever teaching me. You never played sports, you never had girlfriends, I thought you were the strangest kind of older brother. It used to bum me out. And then I got so much taller than you—"

"And it didn't seem to matter so much?" Pete asked.

"Not for a while," said John. "I've been thinking more about it lately, I guess."

The shakiest part of the conversation was over, but the regretful mood left Pete somewhat sullen at his birthday dinner when his niece and nephew helped him blow out all the candles. Grumpy old uncommunicative Uncle Pete was what he felt like.

And now with the news of Lemuel's death and the cars all lined up in the barnyard ready to roll Pete felt gentle waves of sadness breaking over him. He remembered being a little boy by Lake Michigan sitting in the warm sand with his mom when the waves were falling slowly onto the shore. Back then he was an only child. That was what he had heard his Ford grandmother call him in the beach parking lot while he made faces at the fussy mustache of her car. She was talking to his mom as if there was something sad about it but also as if being an only child carried a certain responsibility. Maybe Aunt Helena had been there too. Maybe with Maurice. Maybe it was Maurice who was the only child because at that point Aunt Helena was divorced and would not have another. Maybe Grandmother had been talking to Aunt Helena about Maurice. Pete did not remember. He remembered sitting in the sand with a tin pail and a shovel and looking past the rising waves to the flat horizon. To small Pete it was the edge of the known world.

Pete and Wilfy

Pete was standing in the dusk of the barn. Tomorrow on Labor Day the cars would all be coming home, but today their empty stalls showed only patches of oil on the worn old floorboards where Grampa's horses had once stamped and snorted.

"The children are gone," said Wilfy's dark voice out of the silence. "We got the place to ourselves." He was ambling very slowly toward Pete, one hand thrust deep in his jeans, the other undoing the top button of his blue work shirt. Pete slunk into the Chrysler's stall and flattened himself against the back wall.

In came Wilfy shaking the thing in his jeans. His gray-haired chest emerged as he wriggled out of his shirt sleeves and left the shirt dangling at his pocketed wrist. Pete dodged him and made it as far as the Hudson's stall before he felt big bare arms closing around him, thick

292

fingers struggling with his zipper then yanking his shorts off his ass. "I knew it! No underpants," Wilfy growled, then he whispered in Pete's ear, "I'm gonna give it to ya real good."

He quickly wrestled Pete to the floor and landed him on an old horse blanket Wilfy used when he lay under the cars. Pete could feel the hard cock still in Wilfy's jeans rubbing against his bare butt and pressing him into the blanket. Then Wilfy reached down and pulled Pete's shorts all the way off his gym shoes, and Pete heard the buttons of Wilfy's fly popping open. It was one of their favorite ways to start, Pete in his T-shirt and gym shoes, Wilfy naked to the waist, their skin touching now in only the one place.

Wilfy had grabbed a plastic bottle of motor oil and slicked up his cock and Pete's ass and with his greasy palm reached under to Pete's cock and grasped it tight. He whispered close into Pete's ear, "How's that fer ya?"

Pete nodded. He felt the thick cock rubbing between his butt cheeks, then poking around, then after enough of that, when it was unbearable to wait, Pete relaxed himself and let Wilfy's big warm cock into him. It made his eyes dizzy and blood pound in his temples. After a while he edged himself up on his knees, and then after some of that Wilfy rolled him over on his back to fuck him deeper. Pete forgot what age he was, ignored Wilfy's shortness of breath. They were still pretty good at this.

Then slowly Wilfy lifted Pete up, carried him, held him leaning against the stall divider. Pete reached his hands up to the rail at the top and stretched himself completely into this strenuous fuck. He tightened his thighs around Wilfy's jeans then let go of the rail, his arms tingling, and staggering slightly, puffing but not slipping apart, they were safe on the floorboards again, on the oil patch, Wilfy sweating and steadier and moving slower now to make it last.

quale [kwa-lay]: *Eng. n* 1. A property (such as hardness) considered apart from things that have
that property. 2. A property that is
experienced as distinct from any
source it may have in a physical
object. *Ital. pron. a.* 1. Which, what.
2. Who. 3. Some. 4. As, just as.